the school on
MADISON AVENUE

Books by Ann E. Weiss

Five Roads to the White House

We Will Be Heard
Dissent in the United States

Save the Mustangs!
How a Federal Law Is Passed

The American Presidency

The Vitamin Puzzle
(*with Malcolm E. Weiss*)

News or Not?
Facts and Feelings in the News Media

The American Congress

Polls and Surveys
A Look at Public Opinion Research

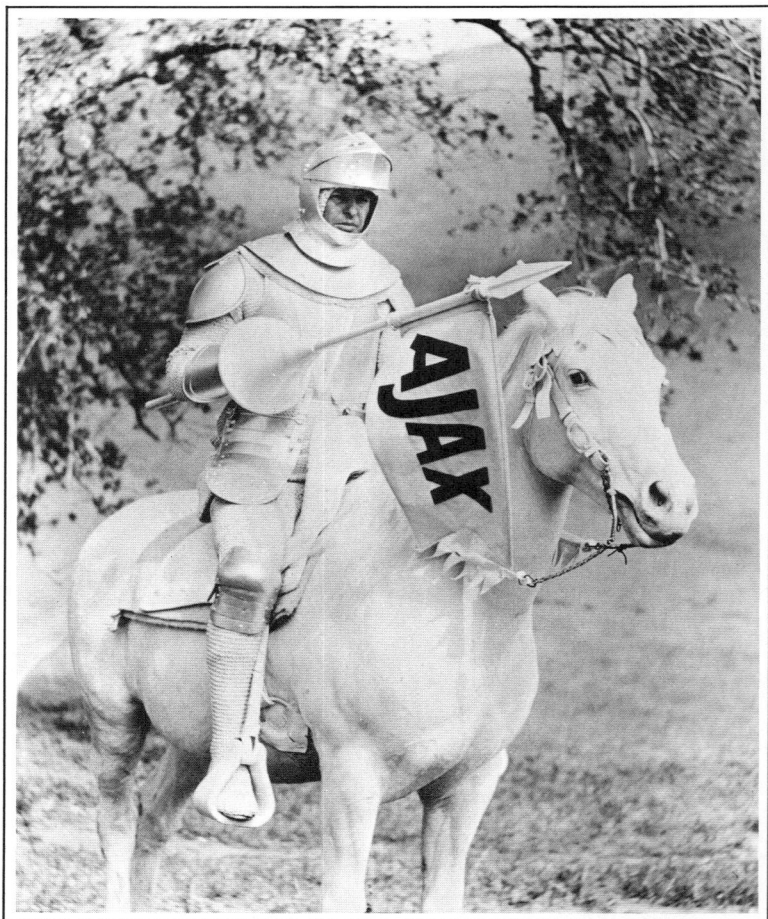

NORMAN, CRAIG & KUMMEL, INC.
FOR COLGATE-PALMOLIVE

The Ajax White Knight—"'Stronger than Dirt''—charged into the life of nearly every American in the mid-1960s.

the school on
MADISON AVENUE

ADVERTISING AND WHAT IT TEACHES

by Ann E. Weiss

illustrated with photographs and drawings

E. P. DUTTON   NEW YORK

Library of Congress Cataloging in Publication Data

Weiss, Ann E., date.   The school on Madison Avenue.
Bibliography: p.   Includes index.
SUMMARY: Discusses the influence advertising has on
our lives for good and for bad.
1. Advertising—United States—Juvenile literature.
[1. Advertising] I. Title.
HF5829.W44   1979   659.1'0973   79-11023   ISBN: 0-525-38823-0

Published in the United States by E. P. Dutton, a Division
of Elsevier-Dutton Publishing Company, Inc., New York
Published simultaneously in Canada by Clarke,
Irwin & Company Limited, Toronto and Vancouver

Editor: Ann Troy   Designer: Meri Shardin

Printed in the U.S.A.   First Edition
10 9 8 7 6 5 4 3 2 1

For Margot, who helped

Author's Note

I am grateful to those companies who allowed me to reproduce their advertisements in this book. Unfortunately, several cigarette companies as well as another advertiser mentioned in the text refused permission to include their advertisements.

Contents

Chapter 1

A Different
Kind of School

Dottie goes to high school in a small town in Vermont. Don is a student at a vocational school in Texas. Kathie goes to a private school for girls in Georgia, and Ken attends a junior high school 3,000 miles away in California.

Yet Ken, Kathie, Don, and Dottie spend hours each week learning together. All four are students at the School on Madison Avenue. So is nearly every other American, man or woman, girl or boy. So are you.

The School on Madison Avenue is different from other schools. For one thing, it comes to its students—not the other way around. We learn its lessons from radio and

1

television. We read them in newspapers and magazines. We watch them at the movies. We see them on billboards, bumper stickers, matchbook covers, T-shirts, beach towels, and buses. We hear them over loudspeakers at the shopping mall and from the salesperson at the front door. We find them in the mailbox and listen to them on the telephone.

The School on Madison Avenue is unusual in other ways. We enroll as babies, and we attend classes all our lives. Lessons go on night and day. We never get a vacation. Yet few of us ever dream that there's a School on Madison Avenue at all.

Is there? There certainly is a Madison Avenue. That's the street in New York City where for years many of the country's largest advertising agencies had their headquarters. Today, some of the agencies have moved to other addresses. But Madison Avenue is still the symbol of the American advertising industry. ''Madison Avenue'' means ''advertising.''

And advertising means teaching. The men and women who work in the country's advertising agencies are paid to teach us. They teach us what products are available for us to buy. They tell us how much those products cost. They inform us about new products. Their messages—the lessons of the School on Madison Avenue—surround us.

Many of their lessons are direct and useful. A newspaper ad tells us that we can save money at a department store sale. TV ads for different brands of cameras let us comparison shop right in our living rooms. A magazine ad for a new cake mix includes a recipe that quickly becomes a family favorite. Ads tell us about movies or TV programs we may enjoy.

Sometimes, ads teach us how to improve our lives. An

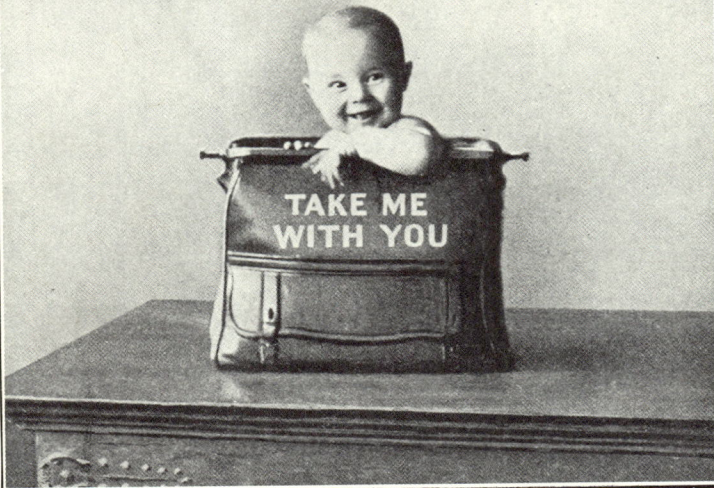

Packer's Tar Soap

TAKE ME WITH YOU

Wherever You Go

TAKE WITH YOU

Packer's Tar Soap

Pure as the Pines

A refreshing cleanser, soothing to irritated skin, antiseptic and—

A Luxury for Bath and Shampoo

THE PACKER MFG. CO., NEW YORK

A good ad can pack a lot into a little space. From this, we learn that Packer's is a pure, refreshing, soothing, germ-killing, luxury soap for hair and skin. This amusing ad appeared in *The Booklovers Magazine* in 1903.

ad from an oil company lists ways we can save energy around the house. Political advertising educates us about the men and women who are running for public office. Ads for convenience foods and electrical gadgets have taught us ways to make everyday life easier and more pleasant.

Other Madison Avenue lessons aren't so direct. On TV, a boy sadly tells his friend that he can't get a girl to go out with him. "Try this!" says the friend, holding out a bottle of mouthwash. The boy rinses his mouth, and next thing you know, he's kissing a beautiful blonde. The direct lesson is that this mouthwash is terrific and everyone ought to use it. The not-so-direct lesson is that loneliness can be cured by purchasing the right product.

Madison Avenue teaches us what other people are like. A neighbor is someone who points out that her hostess's house is dusty or smells funny or that her glassware is spotted. Young girls will jeer at the wife who doesn't get her husband's shirt collar clean. The guy in the next office will let you know when your dandruff offends him. A person could lose her best friend by recommending an inferior brand of shortening.

Besides teaching us about ourselves and other people as individuals, the School on Madison Avenue offers courses on what society is like as a whole. Women are expected to scrub and clean. Men can assume that their wives will cheerfully fetch aspirin for them in the middle of the night. Most Americans are under fifty years of age. Most are white and speak unaccented English.

Some Madison Avenue lessons are harmful in a physical sense. If you're thirsty, reach for a beer or a soft drink. The best breakfast cereal is the most sugary one. Handsome men and beautiful women puff away on cigarettes in

Only the price has changed. For nearly 100 years, Coca-Cola advertising has insisted that Coke drinkers are youthful, attractive, and sure of having fun.

a healthful, outdoor setting. Pills are good for making you sleep, wake up, relax, lose weight, feel happy.

These are a few of the lessons of the School on Madison Avenue. We'll see more later. But first, let's take a look at advertising itself—what it is and what it tries to do.

Chapter 2

Early Days
in Advertising

For eyes that are shining, for cheeks like the dawn,
For beauty that lasts after girlhood is gone,
For prices in reason, the woman who knows
Will buy her cosmetics of—

Of whom? Revlon? Cover Girl? The Avon lady?
The answer is none of these. "The woman who knows"
buys her makeup from Aesclyptoe. Or at least she did
more than 2,000 years ago, when this advertising jingle is
said to have been sung through the streets of ancient Ath-
ens.

For advertising is nothing new. Its origins must go back nearly as far as the human race itself. The caveman who wanted to trade two sharpened flints for a new bone needle had to let his friends know that he was willing to make the exchange. He had to make others aware that he had goods to offer them. He had to advertise. Of course, the caveman didn't call what he was doing *advertising*. He was just speaking up and telling the people around him that he was ready to do business.

Over thousands of years, advertising remained at this primitive one-to-one level. Human communities were small, and it was a simple matter for a person to inform each neighbor individually when he or she had something to buy or sell.

It became less simple, though, when people began to live together in towns and cities. Men and women transacted business at crowded noisy marketplaces. No longer could someone with goods to sell speak to each person who might be interested in buying. Instead, sellers wandered through the market, loudly crying their wares. Or if they could afford it, they hired professional street criers to do the job for them.

One street cry that seems to have survived the ages is Aescylptoe's cosmetic ad. Others remain in traditional songs and nursery rhymes. The old woman who sold sweet rolls cried, "One-a-penny, two-a-penny, hot cross buns!" And the fishwife, proud of her fresh wares, sang, "Cockles and mussels, alive, alive-o . . ." Street criers like these were also known as *hawkers*. From this comes our word *hucksters,* which has changed over the years to mean those who may resort to shady tactics in order to sell their wares.

Like the long-ago caveman, hawkers advertised ver-

During the 1700s, thousands cried their wares through crowded city streets. This London hawker appears to be selling baskets.

bally. Their advertising medium—the means through which they made their sales messages known—was the human voice. But even in ancient times the spoken word was not the only advertising medium. Archaeologists digging through the volcanic ashes that buried the Roman city of Pompeii in A.D. 79 discovered ads painted on the walls of buildings. One, which used words and pictures to announce a gladiatorial contest, promised "slaughter of wild beasts" and "athletic games" as well as awnings to protect spectators from the hot Italian sun.

Art is a universal advertising medium. In medieval Europe, a carved boot overhanging a doorway proclaimed that a cobbler was at work within. Three golden balls arranged in a triangle meant a pawnbroker or moneylender. A pole wound about with red and white stripes was the sign of a barber. Barbers doubled as surgeons, and their striped poles symbolized blood and bandages.

Last names were another advertising medium. A man who called himself Tom Miller was telling people that he would grind their wheat into flour. John Smith was the blacksmith. Bakers, tilers, dyers, cooks, and potters were others who advertised by tacking the names of their trade onto their given names. Last-name advertising wasn't limited to England or to English names. In Germany, Hans Fischer had fish for sale, and Pieter Breuer was the village brewer. In France, Jean Meunier was the miller and Henri Charpentier the carpenter.

But the advertising medium that the people of medieval times must have enjoyed most were miracle plays. Based on Bible stories, these plays were acted before enthusiastic audiences by the members of various guilds. A guild was an association of men who followed the same trade or craft; there was a fishmongers' guild, a wool merchants' guild, a bricklayers' guild, and so on. Since each guild presented the same play year after year, guild members took care to select a story that related to their work. When the Thatchers' Guild put on the Nativity play, for example, the man who played Joseph invariably held up the action in order to deliver a lengthy complaint about the leaky condition of the manger's thatched roof!

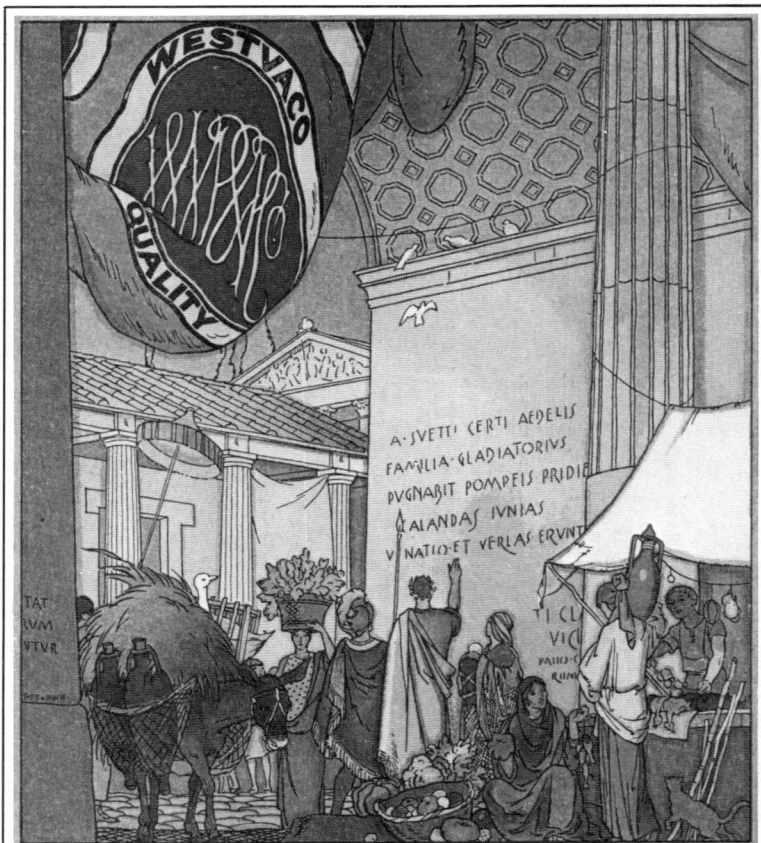

EARLY POMPEIAN WALL INSCRIPTIONS

In the year 79 A. D. the eruption of Vesuvius buried Pompeii. Today in the excavated city its advertising is still visible; wall inscriptions depicting gladiatorial combats, shows, sales, and houses to let. Here perhaps began our bill boards.

A WESTVACO SURFACE FOR EVERY PRINTING NEED

This "billboard" once announced a gladiatorial combat to the people of ancient Pompeii. It was resurrected 1,900 years later for a new advertising campaign.

The invention of the printing press in the 1400s led to great changes in advertising. It became possible to print hundreds of identical copies of an ad and to distribute them over a wide area. Advertisers found this to be a great advantage. A printed ad lasted longer than a verbal one, and it could be handed on from person to person. By the end of the sixteenth century, handbills and posters were advertising everything from the London business school of one Humphrey Baker, to a French merchant's fine silk hose, to the desirability of observing Friday as a fast day on which fish, but not meat, could be eaten. Not surprisingly, the Fishmongers Company paid for the latter ad.

During the seventeenth century, the use of painted advertising grew rapidly. Handbills and posters were still popular. So were advertising pamphlets—each one a glowing account of the virtues of a particular business or industry. But even more important to advertising, the seventeenth century saw the beginnings of the modern newspaper.

Today, the average daily paper contains page after page of advertising. Some early papers, in contrast, carried little advertising or none at all. In 1666, the *London Gazette* declared, "This is to notifie once for all, that we will not charge the *Gazette* with Advertisements." That notice, incidentally, contains the earliest known use of the word *advertisement* to mean the paid announcement of a desire to do business.

But although the *Gazette* shied away from paid advertising, other English newspapers welcomed it. Ads for newly published books abounded. So did ads for "the drink called 'coffee,' or 'cophee'" and for "Tay, alias Tee." Tea and coffee had only recently been introduced to England.

In America, as in England, newspapers and advertising usually went hand in hand. In 1704, the first edition of the earliest successful American paper, the *Boston News-Let-*

ter, solicited advertising from ". . . all Persons who have
Houses, Lands, Tenements, Farms, Ships, Vessels,
Goods, Wares or merchandise, &c to be Sold or Let; or
Servants Run-Away, or Goods Stole or Lost. . . ." That
might seem to have been a complete list of potential advertisers, but the man who has been called "the patron saint
of modern advertising" must have felt that it was just a
start.

That man was Benjamin Franklin. In 1722, when Franklin was sixteen years old, he began his career as a newspaperman and advertiser. He spent 1722 helping his brother
and sister-in-law publish the *New England Courant* in Boston. The next year, Franklin moved to Philadelphia, where
he began to publish his own paper, the *Pennsylvania Gazette.*

Franklin filled the *Gazette*'s columns with ads—ads for
wine, tea, coffee, and other foodstuffs; ads for the return
of runaway slaves and indentured servants; ads for clothing
and for building materials; ads for the sailing of ships; ads
for lost and found items; ads for his own and other people's inventions, and much more. Besides printing more
ads than other publishers, Franklin printed more intriguing
ones. He composed many of the *Gazette*'s ads himself,
displaying a light touch that delighted his readers. One of
Franklin's ads requested the return of his wife's prayer
book, which had been stolen from her pew in Philadelphia's Christ Church. After describing the book, Franklin
concluded the ad with an admonition: "The person who
took it is desired to open it and read the eighth command-
ment, and afterward to return it to the same pew
again. . . ."

Newspaper advertising increased steadily throughout the
1700s. By the end of the century, there were 260 newspa-

pers in the United States. All of them carried some advertising; most carried a great deal. A typical newspaper of the time was four pages long and came out once a week. Its front and back pages were solid advertising, and often two or three columns on another page were given over to ads as well. One Philadelphia paper, the *Political and Commercial Register,* regularly filled at least three-quarters of its pages with ads.

As American newspaper advertising became more common, it grew livelier. Advertisers sought to catch the eye with large or ornate typefaces. "NO PNEUMONIA!" screamed one headline, for the man who wore a Medicated Under Vest filled with a powder that was the Only Safeguard Against Disease. Many ads were illustrated. A Wilsonia Magnet Corset ad included front and back views of a buxom lady clad only in a Wilsonia, which was, the ad promised, "a wonderful remedy for Nervousness, General Debility, Indigestion, Rheumatism and Paralysis."

Extravagant claims for patent medicines were the order of the day. Ads for the "Quassia, or Bitter Tonic Cup," also illustrated, told readers that drinking from the cup would help cure "Sick Headache, Loss of Appetite, Dyspepsia, Fever and Ague, Remittent, Intermittent, and Malarious Fevers, Colic, Sour Stomach, Heartburn, Biliousness, Kidney Complaint, &c." All that for a mere twenty-five cents!

Amusing as these ads seem today, they were taken seriously 150 years ago. People did buy products like the Medicated Under Vests, Wilsonia Corsets, and Bitter Tonic Cups. The ads sold goods, and they did something else. They helped produce the professional advertising agent.

The first American advertising agent was Volney B.

NEW YORK PUBLIC LIBRARY

Exercycles are nothing new—here's an 1896 "exerhorse" that could trot, canter, and gallop! Note that celebrity endorsements aren't new either.

Palmer. Palmer's father was the editor of the New Jersey *Mount Holly Mirror,* and Volney Palmer began his career by getting local business people to buy advertising space in the *Mirror.* He proved to be good at the work, and by 1841, he was doing the same job from an office in Philadelphia. It wasn't long before Palmer opened branch offices in New York and Boston.

Palmer's method was to call on merchants and manufacturers in person to persuade them that advertising—or advertising more—would mean higher profits for them. Palmer cultivated a pleasant manner, which actually concealed a fierce temper, and he generally succeeded in convincing them that they should write more ads and buy newspaper space for them. In payment for his work, Palmer collected a fee, or commission, from the papers in which the businesses advertised. This commission came to 25 percent of the amount the advertiser agreed to pay the newspaper. Today, an advertising agent's commission is usually 15 percent of what the advertiser spends. The commission still comes from the medium in which the ad is placed, not from the advertiser.

Palmer was a success as an advertising agent (until his bad temper gave way to violent insanity), but he never went beyond simply soliciting ads for newspapers. Not so the advertising agents who followed him. They offered another service: *writing* the ads.

The new service caught on at once with advertisers. They were quick to see that an agent who specialized in writing advertising could turn out snappier and more convincing ads than they themselves could. After all, a business person's chief talent is for business, not for writing ads. Advertising agencies multiplied and grew rapidly. Many advertising giants—N. W. Ayer and J. Walter

Thompson, for example—got their starts in these first advertising agencies.

Another reason for the spectacular growth of advertising in the second half of the nineteenth century was that the United States had changed enormously since the American Revolution. In 1790, there were fewer than 4 million Americans living along the Eastern Seaboard. Most were small farmers or artisans—blacksmiths, weavers, carpenters, and the like. Communities tended to be self-contained. Farmers raised crops and sold them nearby. Most people produced their own cloth, soap, candles, and other necessities. When they needed something they couldn't make, a plow or a gun, for instance, they bought the item from a local craftsman they knew and trusted.

A century later, the picture was very different. In 1900, there were nearly 76 million people living in forty-five states from the Atlantic to the Pacific. The average American did not work for himself, but for someone else, usually in a store or a factory. Communities were no longer self-contained; people no longer produced most of what they needed. Food was shipped into cities from faraway farms. Trains carried manufactured goods from eastern and midwestern factories to all parts of the country. Markets were not local anymore—they were national.

Manufacturers couldn't simply advertise in the hometown paper and expect to sell enough to stay in business. They had to advertise in every part of the country where people might buy their products. Advertising had to become national. Thanks largely to a man named Cyrus Hermann Kotzschmar Curtis, it soon did.

In 1883, Curtis and his wife, Louisa, began publishing an eight-page magazine for women. They called it the *Ladies' Home Journal*.

The makers of Pears' soap launched one of the first great modern advertising campaigns. The public loved the choice of illustrations. This was sentimental, but many were amusing.

The *Journal* carried fiction, fashions, child-rearing advice, sewing tips, recipes, and advertising. It was an immediate success, and by the end of 1884, 25,000 women around the country were buying it each month. Fifteen year later, each issue was forty-eight pages long and *Journal* circulation was over a million—an unheard-of figure at that time.

One reason for the *Journal*'s high circulation was its low price, only a dollar for a year's subscription in 1889. Curtis kept the *Journal*'s price down by selling large amounts of advertising space in the magazine. Makers of soap, corsets, toothpaste, and dozens of other products were happy to pay high rates to reach more than a million *Journal* readers every month. The more advertising space Curtis sold, the larger the *Journal* became. Ads helped pay for more editorial matter—stories and articles. The more editorial matter the Journal contained, the more women bought it. And the more women bought it, the more manufacturers were anxious to buy advertising space in it.

"Do you know why we publish the *Ladies' Home Journal*?" Curtis once asked advertisers. "The editor thinks it is for the benefit of American women. That is an illusion . . . the real reason . . . is to give you people who manufacture things that American women want and buy a chance to tell them about your products."

In 1897, Curtis, eager to give manufacturers an equal opportunity to tell American men about their products, began publishing the *Saturday Evening Post*. By 1905, manufacturers and merchants were spending over $1 million a year on *Post* advertising, and five years later, over $5 million. National advertising for national markets was a reality.

By 1910, the pattern of modern American advertising

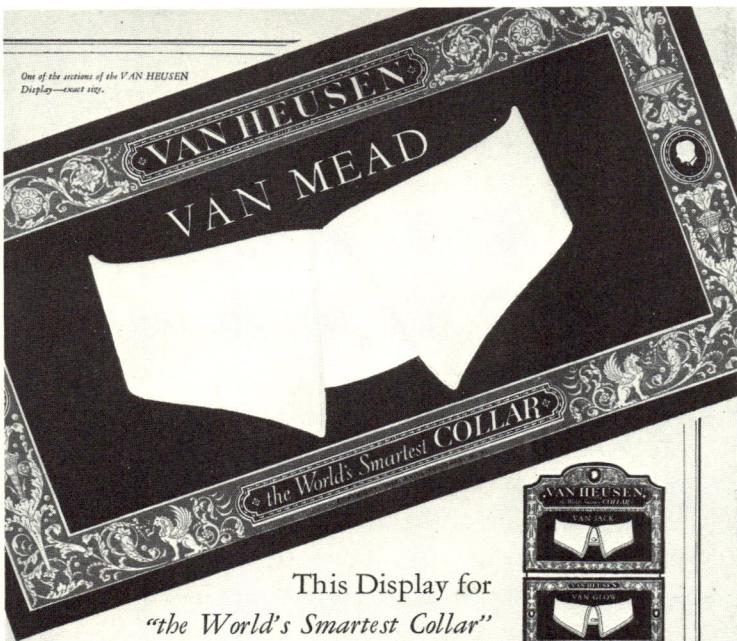

Some ads aim to get advertisers to advertise more. The Powers ad agency wanted to acquaint business people with what it considered its eye-catching work.

was set. Manufacturers realized that they had to advertise in order to sell their products. So they turned to the nation's advertising agencies.

Then, as now, an ad agency employed people with a variety of talents to handle the different aspects of advertising. A researcher could tell the manufacturer—the client—which people would be most likely to be persuaded to buy the product. Another expert could advise the client on which medium would reach the greatest number of those people. For example, if the product were a laundry soap, the most probable buyers would be homemakers, and the best advertising medium, a women's magazine.

Next, an agency copywriter would prepare the advertising message. The copywriter could put the message in the form of a rhyme or jingle, a slogan, a pun, a dramatic vignette—the same forms we are familiar with today. If the ad were to include artwork, an artist at the agency would choose the photograph, or draw the picture or cartoon, or design the package that presumably would sell the product best. Finally, the client would approve the ad, and the agency would place it in the chosen medium.

This arrangement between agent and client worked well, and the early years of the twentieth century were good ones for advertising. Between 1918 and 1929, yearly advertising revenues—the amount of money spent on advertising in a year—leaped from under $1.5 billion to almost $4 billion. Ads for the newly invented automobile, the sales of which more than tripled in the 1920s, accounted for a hefty portion of that increase. So did ads for auto equipment, such as tires; accessories, such as the detachable tonneau to cover riders; and luxuries, such as stylish outfits for the fashion-conscious motorist.

But the automotive market was just one of many new markets that opened with the new century. For the first time it was socially acceptable for women to smoke. Cigarette advertisers gleefully anticipated a doubling of their market. A copywriter for the Lever Brothers soap company wrote an ad warning about "body odor"—and created a market for deodorants. Coca-Cola, first produced in 1886, caught on with the public. Americans began consuming soft drinks by the case load. Houses in most towns and cities had been electrified, and people spent money on all manner of electrical devices.

Suddenly, the boom went bust. The stock market crashed in October 1929, and the years of the Great Depression set in. Millions of Americans lost their jobs, their money, and eventually their homes. Without money, work, or a place to live, people soon stop paying attention to ads that urge them to buy the latest model car, or that threaten social disaster if they don't use the right soap. Business people know that, and as the Depression wore on, most cut down their advertising. Many eliminated it altogether. By 1933, advertising revenues had dropped to below $1.5 billion a year.

Before long, however, advertising began to enjoy a new boom. World War II broke out in Europe in 1939, and two years later the United States entered the fighting. All the country's resources, including advertising, were bent toward victory.

Advertisements urged Americans to join the Army, Navy, Air Force, and Marine Corps. They urged women to become WACS, WAVES, or nurses in the armed forces. They promoted the sale of United States war bonds. They asked people to conserve such vital materials as rubber, fuel, glass, metals, and paper. Many of the ads were paid for by the government, but advertising agencies, the media, and advertisers themselves also donated free time and talent to the war effort.

Advertising got another boost from geared-up wartime

THE OPTIMIST SAYS: "1932 WILL BE BETTER"

THE PESSIMIST SAYS: "1932 WILL BE WORSE"

WE SAY THIS:

Whether business is better or worse, 1932 will be a year of strenuous, stubborn competition. Success, as always, will go to the side with the heaviest sales artillery. To the company that offers honest values . . . that has an energetic sales organization . . . *that obtains the best advertising.*

YOUNG & RUBICAM, INC. *Advertising*

NEW YORK   PHILADELPHIA   CHICAGO

YOUNG & RUBICAM, INC.

When advertising revenues plunged in the Depression, agencies like Young & Rubicam reacted with the theme that business needs to advertise in bad times as well as good ones.

production. Factories could hardly keep pace with the government's demand for all kinds of manufactured goods. American men and women were working again, turning out airplanes, ships, weapons, medical supplies, equipment for the armed forces, and hundreds of other essential items. Workers were making money, and so were their employers. Once more, business people were eager to advertise.

The war ended in 1945, but the advertising boom did not. The raw materials that had gone into making military goods began to go into building hundreds of thousands of new houses. As soon as the houses could be advertised, young families snapped them up. The postwar "baby boom" began, and the birthrate soared. Factories switched from assembling tanks and weapons to producing baby carriages, stoves, and TVs. Americans, their pockets full of wartime earnings, saw ads for such goods and rushed to buy them.

Adults began the postwar spending spree, but the children of the baby boom, entering their teen years, soon joined in. A new market—the "youth market"—had opened.

Today, the market is still growing. In the mid-1970s, boys and girls aged fourteen to twenty-one were earning nearly $50 billion a year—and that doesn't count what their families gave them for allowances. According to one estimate, the average seventeen-year-old had $20 a week to spend.

The average teenager certainly doesn't hesitate to spend. Each year, teens buy a quarter of a million dollars' worth of shampoo. Most records are sold to teenagers. Girls aged thirteen to nineteen spend over $6.5 billion yearly on clothes.

Not only do young people spend billions of dollars of their own money, but they also control much of the spending of their families' money. Who else sends Mom off to the supermarket with instructions to come home with the latest cereal they've seen advertised? Who else gets Dad to bring back a fast-food supper for the family? Who else is given new ski equipment and TVs for their own rooms?

Business has gathered huge profits from the growth of the youth market and from our long spending spree. So has advertising. Today, American business is spending over $48 billion on advertising every year. That amounts to more than $132 million a day—over $1,500 *a second*.

Is the spending of such vast sums necessary? It seems to work. In general, the more a business advertises, the higher its profits.

To those who work on Madison Avenue, though, advertising is more than a way to sell goods. It is a mighty pillar that helps support the American way of life.

Chapter 3

Elementary Lessons

Without ads, we could not live the way we do today. That is something people in advertising never tire of telling us.

In the United States, and in other parts of the world such as Canada and Western Europe, men and women live in a vast sea of consumer goods. Items that would have been luxuries in the past—that are luxuries still to millions of the world's people—are common necessities to us. We would no more think of doing without toothpaste, felt-tipped pens, toilet paper, or deodorant soap than we would of doing without food, clothing, and shelter. People who say they are "trying to make ends meet" have two cars, a color TV, a new set of golf clubs, and an all-electric kitchen. They think nothing of buying a book or record or of dropping in at McDonald's for a snack. Even those Americans who live in poverty—and there are millions who do—are likely to have automobiles and televisions and to eat convenience foods.

How did we come to be surrounded by such luxury? One answer is mass production.

Mass production dates from the Industrial Revolution, which began about 1750. Over the next hundred years, one industrial invention followed another. By 1850, complex steam-powered machines were turning out large quantities of consumer goods.

It's no coincidence that 1850 was also about the time the first advertising agents appeared, for another answer to "Why such luxury?" is advertising.

To see why, imagine that we had mass production but no advertising. Quantities of goods would be produced, but since they would not be advertised, few people would get to hear about them. Fewer would demand to buy them. Soon unsold goods would fill storage warehouses. Manufacturers would stop production. Factories would shut down.

With factories closed, thousands of people would be thrown out of work. They wouldn't be able to afford manufactured goods even if they knew about them. People would return to living as they did before the Industrial Revolution. Farmers and artisans would sell their goods on local markets. Communities would go back to being self-sufficient.

Some people think this might not be such a bad idea. But the point is that it would mean a life-style very different from the one we're used to today. The advertising industry is quite correct about that.

Ad agents are quick to claim that advertising affects our lives in other beneficial ways. By promoting mass production, they say, advertising has kept down the cost of consumer goods. That's because, in general, the more of any item a factory produces, the less it costs to produce each individual item. And the less an item costs to produce, the less the manufacturer needs to charge the consumer for it. Advertising, by persuading people to buy more, encourages manufacturers to produce more. That keeps prices down.

Furthermore, by making many goods available to us at relatively low prices, advertising has helped raise our standard of living. The family that owned one car a few years ago may be able to afford two or three cars now. That makes life easier for Mom and the teenagers. Not long ago, a family was satisfied with one black-and-white television. Today, the same family may have a color TV and one or two black-and-white sets. One family member can watch the feature movie of the evening, and another can see the special on channel five.

Motorboats, camping equipment, and snowmobiles enliven our leisure time. A pocket calculator makes that algebra assignment much less of a chore. Electric freezers and refrigerators keep our food fresh; electric stoves cook it quickly and without mess; electric dishwashers, garbage disposals, and trash mashers make light work of the cleaning up. Such goods, and the advertising that helped produce them, mean an easier and more convenient way of life for all of us.

Agents point out that advertising can lead to a healthier and safer way of life as well. More Americans brush their teeth regularly today than used to before toothpastes were so widely advertised. In fact, we Americans may worry more about cleanliness than any other people. We ought to, inundated as we are by ads for every kind of cleanser, bleach, detergent, scourer, freshener, disinfectant, and scrubber imaginable.

Even our foodstuffs come in sanitary packages, thanks to advertising. At the end of the nineteenth century, an adman designed an eye-catching package for Uneeda Biscuit. Until then, crackers, pickles, flour, sugar, and other foods had been sold ''in bulk'' with customers helping themselves from large tins or barrels. The idea of sanitary, attractive packaging caught on, and now most of the food we buy comes wrapped. Advertisers point out that present-day ads continue promoting new products to keep us safe and healthy. An example is the advertising for home smoke detectors.

Advertising also introduces us to new and useful products and reminds us of products we have fallen out of the habit of using. Ad campaigns for oranges, prunes, and raisins led to enormous increases in the consumption of these foods. Advertising also got Americans to accept frozen foods almost from the moment they reached grocers' shelves. Other products that advertising has acquainted us with include cars, deodorants, fabric softeners—the inventory goes on and on.

Furthermore, say advertising enthusiasts, ads help people feel good about themselves. The girl who wears a lipstick she's seen advertised by a glamorous model feels that some of the glamour has rubbed off on her. A man who drives a Cadillac can feel pleased with himself because ads tell him that a Cadillac is the car preferred by admired and successful men. A boy who dons sneakers that a sports hero claims he uses may have the illusion of running a little faster in them than he would in a different brand.

So far, we've talked about consumer ads, the ads that

are aimed directly at consumers. But there are other kinds of advertising, and they too, say ad agents, benefit consumers.

One kind is industrial advertising. This is directed at manufacturers and appears in the newspapers and business magazines that business people are most likely to read. A large steel company might run an industrial ad aimed at manufacturers of products made with steel, such as automobiles. If the ad gets an automaker to use better or less expensive steel, then that's good for consumers who buy the cars. Another industrial ad might inform clothing manufacturers that a chemical company has developed a new stain-resistant fabric. If that fabric finds its way into the clothes in our closets, we benefit.

Trade advertising is intended for the wholesaler and retailers—the people who buy a manufacturer's products and sell them to the consumer. A dress manufacturer might run a series of trade ads for a new line of tennis clothes, hoping that store owners around the country will read the ads and order those clothes.

Professional advertising appears in publications aimed at men and women doing specific jobs. For instance, a drug company's ad for a new tranquilizer will appear in a medical journal. Doctors who read the journal will see the ad and, drug company executives hope, will remember it the next time they have to prescribe for a nervous patient. Likewise, a publishing company might run ads for school textbooks in a magazine like *Scholastic Teacher* or *Instructor*.

Another kind of advertising is institutional advertising. Institutional advertising does not promote one single item to any one group. Instead, it tries to familiarize people in general with an entire range of products. In a doctor's waiting room, you may see a series of pictures of medical scenes from history: a physician in ancient Egypt; Hippocrates ministering to a patient; Dr. Jenner giving the first smallpox inoculation. The pictures were sent to the doctor by a drug company. They remind everyone who passes through the room, doctors, nurses, patients, worried relatives, of the medical advances of the past—and of the "miracle drugs" they can buy from American drug companies today.

Other institutional advertising comes from business groups with a common interest. Florists want us to "Say It with Flowers." Dairymen tell us that "Milk Is a Natural," and at Christmastime, the Association of American Publishers advises us that "A Book Is a Loving Gift."

Institutional, professional, trade, and industrial advertising benefits consumers by encouraging the production of goods and the development of new products that may turn out to be useful, novel, or amusing. We benefit in a different way from still another kind of advertising, public service advertising.

We saw how during World War II advertising agencies and advertisers volunteered to pay for ads aimed at uniting Americans in the fight. In all, business donated about a billion dollars' worth of advertising between 1941 and 1945. After the war, public service advertising continued. Businesses have sponsored ad campaigns to promote such causes as public education, safe driving, and religion. Often, public service advertising ties in with its sponsor's business interests. A life insurance company might advertise on behalf of supporting cancer research, and a company that manufactures tires might advertise for improved highways. Public service ads run on radio and television as well as in newspapers, magazines, and other media.

Write often to your loved ones, exhorts this institutional ad prepared for the U.S. Postal Service.

Radio, TV, newspapers, and magazines—and those who enjoy them—also benefit from advertising. For, although subscription money covers basic expenses, it's another elementary fact that advertising pays a large part of the costs to maintain those media.

An American soldier, slogging through battlefields of World War II, reminds people at home to do their part and buy war bonds. This was a public service ad.

Advertising allows the commercial networks to broadcast radio and TV programs that are free to those of us who listen to and watch them. It also helps support newspapers and magazines. A hundred years ago, Cyrus Curtis and the *Ladies' Home Journal* proved that advertising and low-cost, high-circulation publications go together. But Curtis wasn't the first to realize that advertising makes it possible for a publisher to put out a periodical at a reasonable price.

In 1831, the editor of the Massachusetts *Springfield Republican,* Samuel Bowles, began to receive complaints about the amount of patent-medicine advertising his paper carried. Bowles lost no time in giving his critics a blunt lesson in economics: "If our readers will agree to give us three dollars instead of two a year for their paper, we will agree to give them one free of advertising." In any case, Bowles pointed out, no one was forcing his subscribers to *read* the ads he printed.

Of course, that's not the situation with radio and TV. We don't have to pay for their programs, as we pay for our newspapers and magazines. But it's harder to escape listening to and watching radio and TV ads than it is to avoid reading ads in print. We "pay" for our favorite shows by listening to their sponsors' messages. Even on public, "noncommercial" TV we frequently hear the announcement "This program has been made possible by a grant" from Mobil Corporation or the McDonald's Local Restaurant Association or some other business. The high quality of today's public TV programming would be impossible without the kind of money that comes from business sponsors.

There are other ways of financing radio and TV. In many European countries, the government pays broadcasting costs for certain stations. Tax-supported networks air a full schedule of news, entertainment, and public affairs programs. There is no commercial advertising on the government stations.

Many Americans wish it were the same here. But advertisers and their agents answer that government should not be so directly concerned with TV and radio broadcasting. It's better for broadcasting to be in the hands of men and women who are independent of the government. Otherwise, what we see and hear might be limited to what the government wants us to see and hear. We might get just one side of the important issues of the day. Advertising people argue that Americans are protected from one-sidedness because our programs are paid for by advertisers with a variety of interests. They say that our commercial system helps safeguard democracy by making sure that many points of view are presented.

Many go further. They say that advertising *is* democracy.

Advertising encourages the mass production of a huge array of consumer goods and tells us that those goods are available. We are free to pick and choose among them. In a way, it's like an election. We "vote" for the products we prefer by buying them. Those products are successful, and the manufacturer goes on making them. The "losers"—the products we don't buy—are no longer produced. That's democracy. The best candidate gets the most votes. The people decide. And advertising makes it possible.

A few people have even equated advertising with religion. In 1926, President Calvin Coolidge told the American Association of Advertising Agencies: "Advertising ministers to the spiritual side of trade. It is a great power which is inspiring and ennobling the commercial world. It is all part of the greater work of the regeneration and redemption of mankind." That same year, a book entitled *The Man Nobody Knows* was a best seller. The book, written by advertising executive Bruce Barton, developed the notion that Jesus Christ was the world's first great adman. If Jesus were alive in the 1920s, Barton claimed, he would have been "a national advertiser."

Not all Americans then, nor all today, would concur with this exalted view of advertising. On the contrary, there are many who attack advertising—and its values and practices—bitterly.

But advertisers have little trouble finding a response to the attacks. "It's not a question if people like advertising or not," says Roger M. Hatchuel, a former advertising director at one large American company. "Advertising is part of our life, part of the system. . . . Whether they like advertising or not is meaningless."

That's elementary—at the School on Madison Avenue.

Chapter 4

Tricks
of the Trade

The word on Project RL came directly from headquarters:

> RL is top secret. Anyone who knows of it must have special security clearance. Discuss the Project only behind closed doors. Commit as little information to paper as possible. When something absolutely must be written down, stamp the document SECRET or EYES ONLY and keep it under lock and key. Destroy papers that are no longer needed in a shredder.

No wonder the brass tried to keep the wraps on Project RL. It was a big-time mission. In a single year, project ex-

penses were expected to run to $50 million. A trained out-
fit of 2,000 agents was being readied to carry out the project's aims.

Then, after years of secrecy, RL's cover was blown.
The R. J. Reynolds Tobacco Company announced that it
was launching an advertising campaign for a new
cigarette—Real.

The campaign's $50 million advertising budget and
2,000 salespeople turned out to be just part of the picture.
During their years of secret preparation, Reynolds officials
had also made plans to hand out more than 25 million free
sample packages of Reals. They had paid for enough dis-
play materials to fill 130 boxcars. They had directed their
advertising agency to rent the largest billboard in New
York City's Times Square for a gigantic ad for the new
cigarette. "Before long," a Reynolds vice-president promised, "you won't be able to turn around out there without
having Real hit you over the head."

The vice-president was right. One newspaper described
Real advertising as "the biggest marketing campaign in
the history of consumer packaged goods."

But Real is not the only cigarette on which millions of
dollars are spent in advertising each year. In a single year,
American cigarette makers spend nearly $500 million for
newspaper and magazine advertising. Advertising budgets
in other industries are similarly high. In one year Procter
and Gamble, which manufactures a variety of soaps and
cleaners, spent $460 million on advertising. General
Motors spent $312 million, and General Foods, $300 million. Revlon paid a comparatively tiny $80 million to ad-
vertise its cosmetics. At the same time, the Ideal Toy Corporation bought $15 million worth of TV advertising time.
The company spent the bulk of that amount in the weeks

before Christmas—a bonanza season for toy makers.

How is this advertising money spent? Much of it goes into preparing the ads we see and hear. For a TV campaign to advertise the Dr. Pepper soft drink, 106 young performers sang and danced their way from California to New Orleans to New York City. To get one twelve-second sequence exactly right, the performers went through seventeen rehearsals and seventy-eight retakes. Finally, the shooting was over. The result—one sixty-second commercial and four thirty-second "spots"—cost nearly $1 million to produce. And that was before any money was spent to air the ads.

The cost of airing an ad, or of getting it into print, is great, too. Sixty seconds of TV time can cost an advertiser $265,000 if it comes during a popular program in evening prime time. On a daytime show with a smaller audience, thirty seconds of time cost anywhere from $6,000 to $20,000. Many advertisers are happy to pay the higher rate for a more popular show because that means more people will see their ads.

Advertising rates in the print media are also based on the popularity of a particular newspaper or magazine and on the number of men, women, or children who will see the ads it carries. A magazine like McCall's, with a circulation of 6.5 million, charges about $44,000 for a full-page color ad. *TV Guide* charges $65,000 for a full-page color ad. Its circulation is over 20 million.

Of course, advertisers are interested in more than just *how many* people see their ads. They want to make sure that the *right kind* of people see them. It's a safe bet that readers of a magazine like *Seventeen* are more likely to buy the newest shade of lipstick than readers of a newsmagazine such as *Time*. So cosmetic makers advertise in

Seventeen, which has only a third of *Time*'s circulation. In the same way, *Time* readers are more likely than *Woman's Day* readers to be in business. That's why you'll find trade, industrial, and institutional advertising in *Time* although its circulation is only half that of *Woman's Day*. *Woman's Day* carries heavy advertising for foods and household products.

Radio and TV advertisers, too, take care to advertise during programs that appeal to the people who may buy their products. Executives at the Lionel electric train company know that often fathers and sons equally enjoy the train sets. So they buy advertising time during TV sports shows and adventure movies—programs that fathers and sons may watch together. The makers of household cleansers have sponsored so many radio and TV daytime serials aimed at homemakers that such programs have been nicknamed soap operas.

Every advertiser, or agent, must be aware of the size and makeup of each advertising medium's audience. Advertising agents must keep track of any changes in that audience. If they do not, they run the risk of wasting the client's advertising dollars. And when those dollars amount to millions each year, waste is unthinkable.

Monitoring their media audiences is only one way people in advertising work to avoid the unthinkable waste. In the country's leading ad agencies, men and women spend long hours laboring over every detail of the ads they prepare. Nothing escapes their notice. Every word in the advertising copy, every line in a drawing, every shadow in a photograph, every note of music—everything must contribute to the ad's overall purpose: making us want to buy the product.

One way an advertiser can get us to buy is by encouraging us to identify with the people we see using the product in the ad. That may make us want to use the product, too. For example, the American Telephone and Telegraph Company paid for a series of TV ads that urge us to call long distance. In one ad, an Illinois woman tells us about her friend who lives in California. The two are close, almost like sisters. How wonderful it is that at a cost of only $2.60 they can talk on the telephone for ten minutes. In another ad, a young mother tells us how she kept her mom informed on the progress of her pregnancy. Naturally, we identify with the people in ads like these. Like them, we have faraway friends and relatives whom we miss. Suddenly, telephoning those we love seems like the right thing to do.

Copywriters can also get us to identify with the people in their ads by placing those people in settings we recognize. In a TV ad for a headache remedy, a harried housewife gazes helplessly around her kitchen. Anyone who's ever done housework sympathizes with this woman's troubles—and feels relief when she swallows a pill and brightens up. Or an ad may show a setting that appeals to our geographic ties. A canned meat could be featured in a southern-style barbecue. People could munch potato chips around a blazing hearth while snow falls gently outside the window. A northerner will feel right at home. For radio and TV ads, actors assume different regional accents to attract listeners and viewers in various parts of the country. One ad is recorded in a midwestern twang, and another for the same product, in a Texas drawl.

Using accents as an advertising gimmick is by no means a new idea. Over a hundred years ago, Thomas Lipton, founder of the Lipton Tea Company, was doing it with great success in Glasgow, Scotland.

Lipton was a born adman. Although he lived in Scotland, his parents were Irish, a circumstance that Lipton found useful when he was a boy working in the family market. Young Thomas took care to speak in either a Scots or an Irish accent, depending on each customer's nationality. In time, he also learned to mimic a number of local dialects. Shoppers felt right at home at Lipton's, where they could hear the accents of their native villages.

When Lipton reached the age of twenty-one, he opened his own market and began advertising it. He had handbills and posters printed up and distributed around Glasgow. He bought a couple of pigs, got them cleaned up and decked out with ribbons, and ordered them herded through the city streets. With the pigs went a banner, "Lipton's orphans." City residents could see for themselves just how superior a porcine family Lipton's hams came from. On another set of pigs, Lipton had painted, "I'm going to Lipton's. The best shop in town for Irish bacon." Glasgow people loved the spectacle and proved it by buying at Lipton's.

Today's ad agents still aim to give their campaigns a touch of Lipton's dramatic flair. The Dr. Pepper extravaganza is an example of their efforts. So was a Chevrolet ad in which a car and a beautiful girl appeared to be perched atop a peak in the Rocky Mountains. Appeared to be? They *were* on the peak. A helicopter carried auto and model to the rocky summit, and an airborne camera crew photographed the scene. In an ad for Schick Easy Rider razor, an actor shaved his face during a demolition derby. "I was terrified," the actor confessed later. "I thought I was going to be killed." But Schick was delighted with its attention-grabbing ad.

Some advertisers prefer to get our attention in less dangerous, less expensive ways. They believe that people

Thomas Lipton had made it big as a tea importer when this ad appeared. His earlier ads may have been less sophisticated, but they were no less entertaining.

identify best with simple, low-key ads. These advertisers may rely on slogans or catchy songs to get their message across. A few business people carry the idea of simplicity to its logical conclusion and make their own ads.

One who does is Tom Carvel, of Carvel ice cream. Carvel doesn't even prepare a script ahead of time. If he makes a mistake, that's okay. "I leave the flubs in deliberately," he explains. "There's nothing like someone saying 'uh, uh, uh,' People relate to this." A New England car dealer advertised on TV by picking up a sledgehammer and aiming a mighty blow at the price sticker on a car window. The dealer made his point, that his customers wouldn't have to pay the full sticker price for a car, without any elaborate staging. All he had to pay for making the ad was the price of the taping session—and the cost of a new windshield.

The advertising techniques we've looked at so far are quite straightforward. They are designed to appeal to us and to make us want a particular product, but they do not attempt to trick us into thinking that the product is bigger or better or more useful than it really is. Other advertising tricks, however, do exactly that.

Thomas Lipton dreamed up one such trick when he was a boy. He suggested that when someone came into the shop for eggs, he and his father should stand aside and let Mrs. Lipton do the selling. Why? Mrs. Lipton had more delicate hands than either her husband or her son. Small eggs looked larger when she held them, and customers thought they were getting more for their money.

The Liptons didn't say anything untrue about the size of their eggs. They just set up a scene that gave a misleading impression and let people draw their own false conclusions. Today, that kind of selling technique has a name— the *permissible lie*.

Modern advertising is full of permissible lies. We're all familiar with ads that tell us: "There's nothing just like Such-and-such." And there isn't. Of course, So-and-so may be identical to Such-and-such, except for its color or flavor or label. That doesn't make the Such-and-such ad a lie, but it doesn't make it the truth either. It makes the ad a permissible lie.

It's easy to learn to spot advertising's carefully worded permissible lies. "No finer kind of . . ." "The unique taste of . . ." "Nothing cleans better than. . . ." But there may be several kinds that are just *as fine*. The taste may be unique, but something else may taste *better*. Many others may clean *just as well*.

Permissible lies come with many disguises. A hand cream that promises a woman it will "keep your hands

"The 'new' on the package—that's what's new!"

The chairman of the board gives his seal of approval to a permissible lie. The "New!" is new. The product is not.

younger-looking" isn't really promising anything at all. Younger-looking than what? Than her hands looked a year ago? Twenty years ago? Younger than they'll look ten years from now? An ad for a tablet that "helps cure your cold" isn't offering you a cure, just a "help." What about a medicine that gives "fast relief" from stomach upset? How fast is "fast"?

Copywriters are clever at using words like *good* and *better* in permissible lies. For years, the Kellogg Company's slogan was "The Best to You Each Morning." Simply a cheery greeting? More than that—a clear implication that Kellogg cereals are the best, and most nutritious, way to start the day. An ad for a cigarette holder said that "nicotine and tars are better in this than in you." True enough. But by the rules of English grammar, that ad says tars and nicotine are *good* in you, *better* in the holder.

An ad can even say that one product is superior to another without using the word *better*. In one commercial, a woman is amazed at how well a particular brand of denture cleaner gets stains off a set of false teeth. She announces that she's going to switch to that brand right away. Without actually saying so, she lets us know that this denture cleaner is better than any other she's used.

Permissible lies can mislead by telling the truth—but not the whole truth. An oil company advertised that its gasoline contained *platformate*. People thought that platformate was a rare ingredient that increased their gas mileage. An ingredient that increased mileage, yes. Rare, no. Platformate, or a platformate-like substance, is part of every refined gasoline. Saying that a gasoline contains platformate, one person commented, "is like a baker advertising, 'I bake my cake with flour.'" An ad for Mazola vegetable oil boasts that Mazola contains no cholesterol, a substance that many doctors believe leads to heart disease. The claim is true enough; but the whole truth is that *no pure* vegetable oil contains cholesterol.

An ad for a pain reliever included the line "Three out of four doctors surveyed recommend. . . ." Perhaps three out of four doctors did recommend that brand. But how many were surveyed? Four thousand . . . or four? Who were they? Independent M.D.'s from reputable hospitals? People employed by the company that manufactured the pain reliever?

A company that makes "squeezably soft" toilet paper began advertising that the paper was now softer than ever. In TV ads, women practically knocked each other out in their eagerness to be the first to squeeze this remarkable product. The toilet paper roll was softer than ever, all right. The manufacturer had made each roll 150 sheets shorter than before and then rolled the sheets that remained so loosely that the roll looked as big as ever. Buyers were spending their money on more squeezability—fewer pieces of toilet paper.

An ad campaign can use other tools besides words to fashion a permissible lie. In a newspaper ad, a huge headline promises great buys at a local shoe store. Only in the small print does it say that the shoes are damaged factory "seconds." On TV, we see a "candid" interview with a consumer who is so devoted to her brand of soap that all efforts to get her to use a different brand fail. The man interviewing her is charmed by her stubborn loyalty. Does the consumer really use that brand exclusively in her everyday life? Well . . . after all, if what she says about the soap pleases its manufacturer, she'll receive a fee for allowing the interview to be broadcast. She'll also have the thrill of seeing herself on TV. And the interviewer is a professional actor who gets a fat paycheck for playing his part.

People can find another form of the permissible lie right in the mailbox. An oversize envelope bears the message "Opening this envelope can make you $100,000 richer!" Sure enough, the people to whom it's addressed learn that they may qualify as sweepstakes winners. They also learn that they're being asked to pay for a subscription to a magazine. Will they have a better chance of winning the sweepstakes if they subscribe? No. But many people assume the answer is yes, and they do send in their money. That's just fine with the advertising people who are running the sweepstakes subscription drive. They don't say a person must subscribe to be a winner, but they may not point out that a subscription isn't *necessary* to win. They don't lie—quite.

Some advertising people, however, do lie. And their lies aren't what even the School on Madison Avenue could call *permissible*. They are just plain lies.

One spectacular advertising lie involved a drug that, its promoters claimed, would allow a person taking it to eat anything he or she wanted to and still lose weight. The drug was called Regimen.

Twenty years ago, Regimen was the hottest-selling diet aid in the United States. That was natural enough since Americans could see for themselves that the drug really did work wonders. Every week on TV, they watched as two plump housewives on the Regimen diet were "weighed in live" on camera. Each week, in spite of having eaten all the potatoes and gravy, cake and candy they wanted, the women weighed less! Doctors appeared on TV to confirm the weight loss and to explain just how Regimen worked.

It was years before the truth came out. The "housewives" were not housewives, but professional actresses. They *had* been overweight. They *had* taken Regimen. They *had not* eaten everything they wanted while on the diet; in fact, they had eaten hardly anything at all. So painful had been their near-starvation diets that each had sought medical treatment. But not from the doctors who had appeared on TV. Those doctors were in the pay of the Regimen company and had received a total of $5,000 to lie about Regimen on the air. Both the company that produced Regimen and the agency that handled its advertising were brought to trial and convicted of fraud.

There have been other cases of outright lying in advertisements. A soup company advertised that its soups were extra-full of meat and vegetables. To demonstrate this on TV, an actor poured a ladleful of steaming hot soup into a bowl. Viewers could see bits of meat and vegetables right on the surface, apparently proving that the soup contained as much solid as liquid. Not until afterward did people discover that all the ad really proved was that the bowl had been half full of marbles when the soup was poured in. The marbles took up enough space to push the meat and vegetables to the top of the bowl.

An ad for shaving cream emphasized the product's marvelous moisturizing and softening power. Applied to sandpaper and allowed to soak in for a moment, the cream softened the paper enough for it to be "shaved" smooth in a single stroke. Actually, through the magic of the TV camera, what appeared to be a moment was nearly an hour and a half of soaking time.

Did that wineglass really shatter when a tape recording of Ella Fitzgerald's voice was played? Yes. But the sound had been magnified to 146 decibels, louder than the human ear can endure and close to the level that can cause damage to other parts of the body. An ad for "distortion-free" glass for car windows certainly got the distortion-free idea across. The ad was filmed with the car window rolled down!

Lies can be found in any advertising medium. Newspapers and magazine ads may echo the false claims of radio and TV advertising for the same products. Other dishonest techniques lend themselves particularly well to the print media. Magazine ads for diet aids often include "before and after" photos. In the "after" photo, the successful dieter's hips may have been "retouched" by an ad agency artist. The result: a woman who looks slimmer than she really is. A newspaper ad for a local store offers color TV sets at "an amazingly low $125." People who turn up to buy the sets are told, "Sorry, we're already sold out. But here's a set for three hundred dollars." The truth is that the store owner never had any sets to sell at the advertised figure. That low price was used as bait to lure customers into the store. Then a clerk tried to switch their attention to higher-priced merchandise. "Bait and switch" is one of the most common of dishonest advertising techniques.

Advertising fraud often crops up in door-to-door selling, too. The young man who says he's working to finance his medical school education may never have graduated from high school. That attractive woman may be collecting for a "charity" that exists only in her sales pitch. The man who tells a recently widowed woman that her husband ordered "this beautiful Bible" just before his death, probably never heard of the deceased until he picked his name from an obituary column.

The Bible salesman lied. But that lie was only part of his selling technique. To get the widow to buy the Bible, he played on her sorrow over her husband's death. Quite literally, he traded on her emotions.

In that, the Bible salesman is like all other advertisers. For, whatever other techniques they use, advertisers know that their most effective selling tool is a successful appeal to people's emotions.

According to one writer, an ad can appeal to the emotions on any of three distinct levels. On the first level are emotions that people admire: patriotism, nostalgia, kindness toward mothers, children, dogs, and so on. On the second level are emotions of which people aren't so proud: inadequacy, guilt, shame, anxiety, alarm, fear. On the third are emotions that few like to admit to: self-interest, ambition, envy, pride, vanity, greed, self-preservation.

Flip through almost any national magazine and you'll find ads that appeal to each of these emotional levels. At the beginning of the magazine, an ad for a hotel chain depicts a peaceful moonlit countryside. From the window of a farmhouse, light streams out into the night. "They left a light in the window. . . . It's the light that will lead you home.'' Pure nostalgia.

Turn a few pages. Gazing out pathetically is a South American child—''doomed to poverty''—unless people send money to the charity that paid for the ad. Only someone with a heart of stone could fail to be touched by pity for this child. That's a level one appeal. At the same time, we begin to think of our own affluent life-styles. Most of us can only guess at the desperation of this child's life. Why do we have so much—and she so little? We're ashamed of our ease and comfort, and we feel guilty. That's a level two appeal.

A few pages farther on is a two-page ad for an expensive blend of whiskey. ''Long after you've forgotten the few extra dollars,'' proclaims the headline, someone will remember that you gave him this whiskey. This is one gift that will make a big impression. Anyone who receives it from you will know that you have good taste—and money to spare. A level three appeal to vanity.

Copywriters don't hesitate to push products by playing on people's secret fears and wishes. As one pointed out, ''The cosmetic manufacturers are not selling lanolin, they are selling hope. . . . We no longer buy oranges, we buy vitality. We do not buy just an auto, we buy prestige.'' Another, criticized for promising that a skin cream would cure all of a woman's complexion problems, demanded, ''What's the difference? Women like to be fooled about the goo they smear on their faces. So we fool them. They love it!''

That's an unflattering picture of the average consumer, but people in advertising seem convinced it's an accurate one. An article in an ad agency newsletter described the emotional state of a typical supermarket shopper. To the

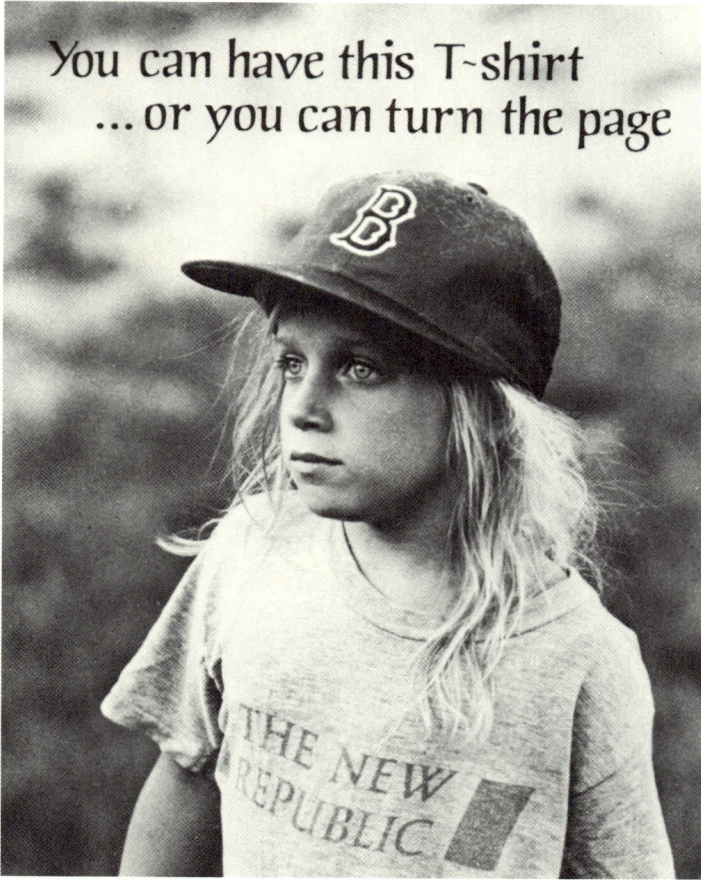

ANNE PERETZ/THE NEW REPUBLIC

In a series of ads for a foreign charity, photos of mournful children are used to appeal to vague feelings of guilt. This parody appeals to a sense of humor.

shopper, the supermarket was "one grand shout." As she selected a shopping cart, her "pulse rate and respiration changed. She was poised like a cat, ready to spring when she saw something new and better. Quicker. Tastier. Newer. A better buy. A handier spout. A more promising promise."

Frank as copywriters may be among themselves about trying to appeal to people's emotions, they are less anxious to let the public know that that's what they're doing. On the contrary, many conceal the emotional appeal of the ads they write.

How does this concealment work? Take a TV ad for a headache remedy. As the actors in the commerical talk about fast relief, soothing music plays softly in the background. On Madison Avenue, this kind of music is called a *rug* or *carpet*. A person watching the commercial may hardly be conscious of the music. But subconsciously, it's different. Scientists know that the subconscious mind takes in far more impressions every second than does the conscious mind. Experiments prove that the human subconscious notices and remembers nearly every detail of every event of a person's life.

So there the viewer sits, barely noticing the ad. But with his subconscious mind, he hears and remembers every word, every note of music. In his subconscious, the name of the headache remedy is linked with the gentle soothing quality of the music. Days later, when he has a headache, his subconscious memory may direct him to select that medicine for relief.

In another ad, the musical appeal to the subconscious may not be soothing at all. Suppose the ad is for a patent medicine that "helps cure" colds, muscle aches, or stomach upsets. The *rug* sets the stage by reminding the viewer of how awful such ailments can make him feel. The music sounds eerie, discordant. It irritates. One composer of advertising music, Suzanne Ciani, explains why: "The motivation in this type of music is to produce the discomfort and the tensions, however subconsciously, in the viewer."

Midway through the commercial, the name of the distress-relieving product is mentioned, and the music changes. It calms, soothes. "The relief comes at the point where he [the viewer] knows he was uncomfortable," Ms. Ciani continues. "He may not realize it at the time. You try to induce that reaction."

Lighting technicians, too, work to induce that reaction. At the beginning of the cold-medicine ad, the scene may appear dull, murky. When the music changes, so does the lighting. Once the remedy is swallowed, everything brightens up.

Color can also be used to appeal to our subconscious minds. Compare a magazine ad for a children's medication to one for some kind of hard liquor. Chances are soft pastels will dominate in the former; dark, bold, dramatic colors in the latter. Ads for household cleaning products—soaps, detergents, and polishes—typically feature clear, bright tones with lots of clean white space. The colors in ads for products like clothes and cosmetics conform to changing fashions—glowing one year, muted the next.

The props that appear in an ad may be designed to appeal to our subconscious selves, too. The focus of a full-page magazine ad for a dishwashing soap is a woman's reflection shining on a plate that has theoretically been washed in the liquid. A headline in inch-high type, "See it for yourself," appears across the top of the page. A photo of the soap bottle is prominent at the bottom right-hand corner.

On a conscious level, that's about all the average magazine reader will notice in this ad. Yet as the reader turns the page, she may smile slightly or feel her spirits rise. Why? Her subconscious mind, which takes in many times the number of details that her conscious mind does, has noticed the small photo above the bottle of soap. A festively set table . . . gold cloth and napkins . . . blue plates sparkling clean . . . a carved roast . . . corn on the cob . . . rolls. An attractive young woman is just setting out the salad. Around the table are another woman, two men, and two children.

To our reader's subconscious mind, that's a picture of sheer delight—at least so the person who wrote the ad hopes. The reader, of course, is supposed to identify with the attractive hostess. It's her husband who gazes attentively at her from across the table and their closest friends who are about to share her delicious dinner. Those are her well-mannered children, the little girl sitting with her hands politely folded in her lap, the baby quiet in his highchair. Naturally, our reader smiles. Part of her mind—a hidden part, but a part nonetheless—has caught a glimpse of an idyllic family scene. And this idyll is associated in her subconscious with a particular soap. Next time she goes to the supermarket her subconscious may prod her to buy that soap—and an image of domestic bliss.

If an agent can get so much across in a magazine ad, what can be accomplished in a sixty-second TV commercial? Plenty. Think of all the inviting little vignettes of harmonious family life we see in TV ads. And think of all the other visual appeals to our subconscious minds that are worked into television ads. The spotlessly neat kitchen in an ad for shortening. The beautifully dressed children in an ad for cat food. The happy faces of the women who scrub and clean with one product after another. The obviously expensive house that belongs to a man about to come down with an achy cold. The old-world village scene that implies that made-in-America Lowenbräu beer is really brewed in Germany.

Many people don't want to believe that agents try to sell products by appealing to our subconscious minds. Even if they tried to do so, people argue, it wouldn't work. The human mind simply can't take things in so quickly. It can't recognize all the details of a picture, all the color clues, all the notes in a piece of music that it would have to recognize for a subconscious appeal to do its job.

That sounds like a good argument. But we have frightening evidence that it may not be.

About twenty years ago, a device called a *tachistoscope* came to public attention. A tachistoscope is a film projector with a super-high-speed shutter. Every five seconds, it flashes an image upon a screen. That image is visible for only $^1/_{3,000}$ of a second. The tachistoscope was originally developed by scientists exploring the human mind. Today, it is used to help teach children to read.

But Madison Avenue came up with a different use for the machine. Advertising agents pioneered that use in a Fort Lee, New Jersey, movie theater.

While the movie was going on, the tachistoscope flashed out messages: "Hungry? Eat popcorn" and "Drink Coca-Cola." The messages did not interfere with the movie, and no one in the theater was consciously aware of having seen them. Yet when the movie ended, people poured into the lobby to buy popcorn and Coke. In a six-week test of the tachistoscope, Coke sales in the theater increased 18.1 percent, and popcorn sales, 57.7 percent.

When the public learned the facts, it raised an outcry

"*They must be using one of those hidden commercials. I suddenly feel a terrible urge for something called O'Brien's Mustard Pickles.*"

Has this woman been "sold" on a product through her subconscious mind? Thanks to the tachistoscope, it can happen.

against the use of the tachistoscope in advertising. Bills were introduced in Congress to outlaw the device. None became law. As far as we know, the tachistoscope is not being used in advertising today. But the experiments with it serve as a reminder that advertising appeals to our subconscious minds *can* be successful.

That kind of advertising strikes many people as underhanded. But there's another kind that is just as underhanded. Maybe even more so. It is called public relations.

Of course, not all public relations is sneaky. Public relations refers to the efforts of a business or an institution to build good will among customers or the public. For instance, a high school principal might try to get information about up-coming school events into the local newspaper. The principal's aim is to maintain friendly, open relations between the community and the school. That's a laudable public relations goal. Or a supermarket chain may inform the news media about a scholarship program it is sponsoring. Such a program is PR at its best—it benefits students and makes the supermarket chain look good at the same time.

But other public relations efforts are not so well intentioned. Much of the PR material we see, hear, and read is simply advertising in disguise. One example appeared in headline form in the *Christian Science Monitor,* a newspaper that is read all across the country. According to the *Monitor,* Macy's department store in New York City was to be a shooting location for a popular TV actress's first motion picture. Here are some other things this six-paragraph story told its readers:

Macy's, located in Herald Square, is a bustling nineteen stories high—"the world's largest store."

Macy's has had more than its share of movies, including the classic *Miracle on 34th Street,* filmed there.

Macy's huge balloon floats, a feature of New York City's annual Thanksgiving Day Parade, are stored in a Hoboken, New Jersey, warehouse.

Macy's calls the movie "a fun, family, and escapist kind of movie."

Macy's says, "Macy's is a family store and this is very much a family movie."

Macy's "adores" the crowds that shop there.

If Macy's had had to rely on advertising to get all this information across to the public, it would have cost a pretty penny. Even if an ad agent had managed to work all those separate facts about Macy's into a single one-page ad in the *New York Times,* the store would have had to spend thousands of dollars on the newspaper space alone. More likely, an agent would have had to write two or three individual ads. Costs would have soared. Fortunately for Macy's, no advertising was necessary. Newspapers printed all the information for free. Perhaps more New York area shoppers read that story than would have read a complete Macy's ad in the *Times*.

The Macy's case is far from unique. Our news media—newspapers, magazines, radio, and TV—are filled with public relations "puffery." A newspaper article says that the phone company wants to charge customers new, higher rates because of rising costs. Nowhere in the article is there any criticism of the proposed new rates. That's because this "news story" is a press release from the phone company. The newspaper editor may have printed the release just as it came from the phone company or have asked a young reporter to reword it slightly. In either case, it's public relations.

A radio report says that the electric company plans to build a nuclear power plant in your part of the state. There's no reference to the known hazards of nuclear power. On TV, a film shows lumber company workers planting seedlings to replace logged trees. The sight makes viewers think favorably of the lumber company. Perhaps their attitude would be different if the report also mentioned that the amount of money the company spends on reforesting is a tiny fraction of its profits. But that sort of information has no place in this report, which was written and filmed by the lumber company's public relations department.

Public relations puffery even makes its way into American schools and classrooms. "Tony the Tiger" breakfast food posters grace many a school cafeteria wall. Tony is cute—and a constant reminder of Kellogg's sugar-coated cereals. A tobacco company offers pamphlets that urge students to believe that the sale of cigarettes is central to the country's economy. "Cigarettes and civilization: The two seem to go together . . ." the pamphlets begin.

A publication from a meat producers' group teaches that because the American Indians were a hunting people, they could never have progressed as far as the Europeans, who settled down and domesticated animals to use for food. Other PR material that is found in schools comes free of charge from power companies, car manufacturers, cheese processors, soft-drink makers, and so on.

Advertising in the guise of public relations—like the advertising that appeals to our subconscious minds, is sneaky because it catches us unaware. It urges us to spend money, or to think well of a company or its products, without any warning that's what it is setting out to do. This kind of advertising does not give us a chance to think rationally or critically about the messages it presents. The people who sipped Coke and munched popcorn in a certain Fort Lee theater years ago can testify to that.

It is important that we try to look at disguised advertising, indeed at all advertising, carefully and critically. We should always look at it with the question in mind "What is this ad really saying?"

Chapter 5

Lessons
in Living

How much have we learned at the School on Madison Avenue? Just consider: By the time most Americans are eighteen years old, they have spent 12,000 hours in school and 15,000 hours in front of the TV set. From the age of about three on, they have watched TV between 25 and 30 hours a week, every week of the year. During those hours, they have seen a full five hours of commercials. In other words, American students spend more time each week watching TV ads than they do listening to their math or English teacher.

And television is only one advertising medium. Most

teenagers read a newspaper each day. They may turn first to the news and to the comics and "Dear Abby," but they take time to study the ads for movies and record store sales, too. Readers of magazines like *Glamour* and *Sports Illustrated* may give as much time to looking at ads for clothes and outdoor equipment as they do to reading the magazine's stories and articles. People get into their automobiles only to be confronted with ads mounted on billboards, flashing neon signs, painted on buildings, and printed on trucks and vans. They turn on their car radios and hear still more ads. On some stations, radio advertising regularly amounts to eighteen minutes out of every hour of broadcasting time.

In a book called *The Art of Advertising,* authors George Lois and Bill Pitts say that the average American is exposed to 1,500 advertising message a day. Certainly, we students at the School on Madison Avenue are given every opportunity to learn our lessons thoroughly.

What, exactly, do we learn? Many lessons concern the English language.

Take spelling. *Quick* has become q-u-i-k or k-w-i-k. *Night* is n-i-t-e, *bright* is b-r-i-t-e, and so on. *Stay* is spelled s-t-a; *doughnut,* d-o-n-u-t; *tough,* t-u-f; and *clean,* k-l-e-e-n. Such spelling is E-Z to remember. Recently a third-grade class was asked to spell the word *relief.* Over half the class answered "R-O-L-A-I-D-S."

Or take the meanings of words. What is *big* compared to *bigger, biggest, jumbo, super, mammoth, colossal,* or *supercolossal?* Pretty small, that's what *big* is. Similarly, *new* ages fast as *newer, newest, all-new, new improved, new-new, and new-new-new* fill the shelves.

When children are six or seven years old, they learn that every minute lasts sixty seconds. But in ads, minutes are "short" when it comes to the speedy relief we can expect from patent medicines, "long" when it's a question of the enjoyment to be had from a cigarette or a stick of gum. Pints, pounds, and miles all change in size, weight, and length depending on what is being advertised.

It's not just a matter of stretching word meaning either. Sometimes we hear entirely new definitions. In a radio ad for a northern New England dairy, a young woman gaily informs listeners that, "I have a real phobia about freshness, and I'm proud of it!" She goes on to rave about the freshness of the dairy's milk and cheeses. The people who dreamed up that ad ought to look up *phobia* in the dictionary and ask themselves why anyone should be so delighted about having an irrational fear of fresh dairy products.

We learn new grammatical constructions from ads, too. A message on a cereal box urged children to send in two box tops and $1.50 to receive "A fun cap to warm up winter days." What's a fun cap? A cap that's having fun, perhaps. An ad for Zest soap promises that Zest "will leave you cleaner than your soap." Cleaner than *soap?* And the word *like* has forever replaced *as* as a conjunction, thanks to cigarette advertising that insisted, "Winston tastes good like a cigarette should."

Other ads teach manners. Ad show parents and children alike chewing with their mouths open and talking with their mouths full. People interrupt each other at will, and *please* seems to be a forgotten word. Even more startling are ads that show people doing in public things that used to be considered strictly private.

Turn on the TV, and there's someone taking a shower. Right in your living room! People bathe, brush their teeth, gargle, use mouthwash, and apply deodorant before our very eyes. Men shave their faces, and women, their legs and underarms. Women model their pantyhouse, exclaiming as they do so at its comfort and durability. People unblushingly discuss the merits of a host of intimate products. A few ads go to the extreme of encouraging nudity. Wearing a certain brand of panty hose "makes you feel like you're not wearing nothing." The grammar is confused, but the message is plain.

Ads also instruct us about the kinds of problems we can expect to face in our daily lives. They paint a grim picture.

Dad can hardly drag himself out of bed. Mom wakes up with a sore throat and throbbing corns. Paul is faced with a new brand of cereal. Melissa's sweater reveals evidence of dandruff.

Dad cuts himself shaving with an inferior razor and suffers a bout of indigestion. Mom gets Paul to eat his cereal (he loves it!) but uses a thin, watery pancake syrup. Melissa is suddenly stricken with the knowledge that, as a woman, she is flirting with an iron deficiency.

But enough of the problems of Mom, Dad, Melissa, and Paul. Their troubles are minor ones, the kind that ads are eager to warn us about. The threat that we share such problems is an explicit lesson of Madison Avenue.

Underlying it are lessons about more serious problems— feelings of insecurity, of helplessness, of fear. Ads don't tell us directly about such problems. They are not the focus of most of the national advertising we see and hear. They are the hidden, implicit lessons of advertising.

How do we learn them? One way is by hearing over and over about our failings and limitations.

Think for a moment about the things some ads tell children about themselves. Children are messy, dirty nuisances. They leave muddy towels in the bathroom. They track up newly waxed floors. They come into the house howling over small cuts, and they fuss when bandages are removed. They greedily devour anything that is sugary, gooey, chewy, crunchy, juicy, or yummy. Repeatedly, ads show children that they are not really very nice people.

Ads tell women a lot about themselves, too. For one thing, women discover that they have some rather disagreeable characteristics. In one newspaper ad for a New York City department store, a sleek cat posed with a cigarette holder and an elegant hat. The headline read: "I found out about Joan." What the speaker "found out" was that Joan and her husband were in debt up to their ears and Joan managed to dress in the latest Paris fashions only because she shopped at this particular low-cost store.

This ad gained a brief notoriety when it came under discussion on television's "Today" show. "Today" hostess Jane Pauley questioned admen about the ad's implications. Doesn't it depict women as cats? she wanted to know. And doesn't it suggest that women are cruel and gossipy? "So what?" retorted one guest. "Many are." A fellow agent backed him up. "We're truthful and honest," he told the outraged Ms. Pauley.

Actually, ads like this one, ads that show women as smartly dressed people of the world, are not common, except in fashion magazines. In most ads that feature women, the women are homebodies. They cook. They clean. They sew. They worry about what diaper absorbs best. They seriously debate the merits of various brands of laundry soaps.

Unlike Joan and her backbiting friends, these women are good creatures. Their main purpose in life is to work to make their families comfortable. "Nothing's too good for Daddy and me," sings one little boy. "Mom brings Del

Monte home." Mothers in ads serve their sons and husbands, and they bring up their daughters to do likewise.
Ads for Ortega tacos ask, "Which is more fun, making
Ortega tacos or eating them?" In most of the ads, husbands and children answer, "Eating them." But mothers
and big sisters disagree. "Making them!" they chorus
happily.

The women in these ads may be sweet and generous,
but they are not very bright. They require constant coach-
ing as they go about their daily chores. Women scrub and
cook while off-screen male voices tell them what's right—
and wrong—about the way they work and the products
they use.

In one ad a man told a young wife just how to bake a
loaf of bread. As he named each ingredient, the woman
obediently dropped it into a bowl. There are rare cases,
though, when a man urges a woman to strike out on her
own. Why, a man's voice exclaims, just by adding water
to a prepared powder, a woman can make her own ar-
tificial whipped cream! After watching a few hundred ads
like these, you realize that a woman can do practically
anything—as long as she has a man around to tell her how.

Women had better watch out though. They're safe only
until they reach the age of forty-nine. Women older than
that are seldom seen in ads.

Neither are older men. "The television industry retires
us all at age forty-nine," complains Nicholas Johnson, a
former member of the Federal Communications Commission, which regulates radio and TV.

Johnson exaggerates. The middle-aged and elderly
aren't eliminated from advertising, on TV or anywhere
else.

But when we do see older people in ads, it's usually

made clear that they have worse failings and limitations than women *or* children. The very products they advertise—painkillers, laxatives, and denture cleaners, for instance—are a reminder of the bodily miseries that old age may bring. Old age means other problems as well. In a Jell-O ad, a grandmotherly-looking person can't remember whether or not she made a pudding a couple of hours earlier. The poor woman is about sixty years old—and senile. Ads tell us that to be old means to be deaf, to have trouble getting up or walking about, to act confused, and to be ridiculous.

There are other groups that many ads portray in a poor light. Mothers-in-law are nosy and critical. Teachers are stuffy. The boss is pompous. Unmarried women are thin and unattractive old maids. Advertising did not invent these stereotyped ideas about people, but it doesn't hesitate to use them. Copywriters know that we all recognize such stereotypes. They hope that we will react to them in a predictable manner.

We accept the idea that a mother-in-law will barge into her new daughter-in-law's kitchen and offer advice on the best kind of tomato paste to use in spaghetti sauce. Accepting this stereotype is supposed to lead us to accept the advertising message that goes with it—that this tomato paste is superior to all others.

Criticism, such as the mother-in-law's criticism of the young wife's cooking, is a common advertising theme. In ads, people do a lot of criticizing of other people. People inform their co-workers that they have bad breath or dandruff. A son scolds his mother for serving a soggy piecrust to his fiancée. A child whispers to her mother that her friend's towel doesn't smell very good. A husband complains that his wife didn't get his shirt clean enough.

Women mutter about a neighbor's dirty floor behind her back. Everyone on the block is struggling to be cleaner, blonder, younger-looking than anyone else. People know they must have the newest car, the softest hands, the crunchiest fried chicken, or they will be talked about, criticized, and condemned.

And how desperate they are to avoid such a condemnation! In an ad for Dodge cars, a man awakens his wife at 4:00 A.M. with instructions to "start packing, dear." "Dear" wants to know why. Her husband explains that they are the only ones on the block without a new Dodge. "I'm so ashamed," he mourns.

This is an amusing ad—taken by itself. But remember that by one estimate, Americans see 1,500 ads a day. And many of them, like this Dodge ad, seek to persuade us that we have more needs and problems than we ever imagined.

Once upon a time, for instance, people thought that if they washed themselves daily with soap, they would be clean. Then ad agents began writing about body odor, and people decided that they needed a deodorant as well. For a while after that, people drifted along, assuming they were no longer offending anyone. Not so! Suddenly they found out they had to wash with a bacteria-killing soap before using a deodorant. Were people now clean enough? Men apparently were. But women needed still more deodorizing, as TV and magazine ads rushed to inform them.

It's amazing the number of things we didn't use to know we needed. Microwave ovens. Colored kitchen appliances. Bucket seats, reclining seats, whitewall tires. Potato chips that stack in a can. Rippled potato chips that stack in a can. Scented mouthwashes. Dolls that change from brunette to blond with a twist of the head. Electronic games to play on the TV screen.

THE BETTMANN ARCHIVE

Today it's "bad breath" or "medicine breath." Older ads were more blunt. But by any name, the advertiser claims the problem means loneliness unless you buy the right product.

We lack so many things. So much criticism is leveled at us. We have such severe limitations. By now, we may begin to suspect that the world is an extraordinarily unfriendly place. We may feel more and more helpless in it.

That's just how we're supposed to feel.

For having shown us that we must struggle against a hostile world, advertising teaches us how to survive in that world. It shows us how to feel better about ourselves. It helps us silence the criticisms of others. It teaches us to bolster our sagging self-esteem.

How? By giving us the chance to own all those wonderful products that ads assure us are making everyone else so happy and secure.

One thing advertising offers us is food and drink. Just as a mother gives a bottle to her wailing baby, so advertising agents suggest that the physical gratification of eating and drinking will help still our doubts and anxieties. "You deserve a break today," says the McDonald's ad. The implicit message is that food is a reward you should give yourself when you need cheering up. This message is underscored by massive advertising for unessential, unnourishing foods. Only 2 percent of all the food ads aimed at children are for meat, bread, fruits and vegetables, or dairy products. Cereal ads emphasize sweet taste and attractive appearance. Says one critic of American breakfast foods, Robert Choate, cereal ads "advise . . . children to equate sugar with health and snacks with happiness."

But suppose that eating and drinking aren't enough to make people forget that they're unhappy or insecure. Advertising has other possible solutions:

Using this brand of toothpaste keeps a child from getting cavities. His parents are delighted. They show their delight by hugging and kissing him. *This toothpaste equals love.*

Using this shampoo makes a girl's hair smell so great that everyone in the office asks her enviously how she keeps it so fresh. *This shampoo equals superiority.*

Using this polish makes a woman's house shine so that her friends gasp in amazement. *This polish equals admiration.*

The people who write ads like these are selling more than products. They are selling people good feelings about themselves. They are suggesting that people can solve problems—serious problems of loneliness, self-hatred, unhappiness—by using certain products. They are suggesting that money *can* buy happiness.

Ads offer other solutions for people who feel insecure. They tell people that they don't have to stand alone. They can go along with the crowd, instead, and find safety in numbers. All they have to do is buy America's fastest-selling car, its most used pill, its favorite flavor, its leading detergent. If everybody's doing it, then no one can criticize anybody else for doing it, too. One friend tells another about Bounce fabric softener. Soon the whole neighborhood's using it. Everyone's clothes are equally soft and fresh. Everyone is happy. Or people can drink Pepsi and become part of an entire generation. They'll never be alone again.

A leading adman of the early twentieth century, Claude C. Hopkins, thought the going-along-with-the-crowd lesson was advertising's most powerful tool. "People are like sheep," he said. "They cannot judge values; neither can you and I. We judge things largely by others' impressions, by popular favor. We go with the crowd. The most effective thing I've ever found in advertising is the trend of the crowd."

People are like sheep . . . they go with the crowd . . .

they are not strong enough to act alone . . . they dare not stand up for what they like or believe in. These, too, are among the lessons of Madison Avenue, and few people are consciously aware of hearing them. These lessons are very different from the ones that most of us consciously learned from our families, our teachers, and our religious leaders. The traditional lessons, like "Dare to be different" or "Stand on your own two feet," are rare in ads.

There are other advertising messages that strike at the root of much of our moral training. Our parents may have told us that happiness comes from within ourselves. Happiness will be ours if we do what we know to be right, if we obey the Golden Rule. Happiness depends on what we *are*.

But in ads we hear that we can be happy if we buy this or that. Happiness depends on what we *own*. "Such callous debasement of what constitutes happiness," says one psychiatrist, "must weaken the traditional American concepts of high ideals, especially with the very young."

Ads have something to say about home life, too. Ask most people what a home is, and they will tell you that a home consists of a father, a mother, or both, several children, and perhaps grandparents. In other words, they define *home* in terms of people. Some ads offer a different definition. Home like happiness, is a series of products. General Electric stoves and refrigerators—The Appliances America Comes Home To—make a home.

People used to be taught to be careful of their belongings, to make things last. But much modern advertising tells people to eat it up, use it up, wear it out—and replace it with a new, improved model.

Self-denial was once thought of as a virtue, but many ads discourage it. "You deserve a break *today*," the ad

"Frankly, S. L. — I think it stinks!"

One of the first principles of Young & Rubicam, and one that's lasted, is the firm conviction that "brass hat" doesn't mean brass knuckles. The newest employee can argue with the oldest ex- ecutive—and win, if merit is on his side. There isn't a shadow of doubt that an agency—and its clients—profit most from a man's mind when he feels free to express his honest convictions.

YOUNG & RUBICAM, INC.
Advertising • New York Chicago Detroit San Francisco
Hollywood Montreal Toronto Mexico City London

YOUNG & RUBICAM, INC.

Young & Rubicam still advertises to advertisers. Here the message is: We dare to be different. We will write honest advertising copy for you.

tells us. You also deserve a moped, a sit-down mower, a trip to Mexico, and a new dress for the prom—and you deserve them all right now.

Life should be easy as well as pleasant. Ads for labor-saving devices fill page after page in newspapers and magazines and hour after hour on T V and radio. Many of these devices are very much worthwhile. Few people would suggest that we ought to abandon our washing machines for scrubboards or scythe the lawn instead of using a power mower on it. But what about a polish that is sprayed on furniture instead of being poured onto a cloth before rubbing? Is that really such a gain? It is for anyone who has thoroughly absorbed the idea that we must take advantage of anything at all that will make life even a tiny bit easier.

By the time we've learned to accept ease and to reject self-denial, another lesson—that we should always put ourselves first—comes naturally. We can forget that we ever learned such sayings as "Do for others" or "Others first, myself last." We should try to please ourselves first of all.

After all, "You, you're the one." You should take a patent medicine at the first twinge of pain, so you'll never suffer. Mom wants you to eat a nutritious breakfast, so here's a cereal that will please *you*—it's sugary and crunchy and turns the milk in your bowl into chocolate milk. McDonald's sums it up neatly, "We do it all for you-u-u-u. . . ."

Most parents try to teach their children that telling lies is bad. But the message we get from some ads is that lying is kind of cute. In a Duncan Hines ad, a mother leaves daughter Janie to keep others in the family from eating a cake before it's frosted. Alas, Janie falls prey to temptation and eats some of the cake herself. When her father appears, Janie confesses.

Now father could do one of several things. He could tell Janie firmly that she ought to have obeyed her mother. He could bawl Janie out. He could send her to her room or deprive her of dessert. Instead, father finds he can't deny himself the forbidden cake either. Mouths crumby, Janie and her father giggle together, equals in disobedience.

What does this imply? That we have no one to look up to, no one to tell us that right is right and wrong is wrong. This idea is driven home in scores of ads that picture traditional figures of authority—policemen, military officers, clergymen, teachers, parents, older people—as foolish, priggish, dishonest, or immature.

A panty hose ad shows a black-robed judge ogling a girl's legs. Judges in another ad disrupt the court as they gulp Doritos tortilla chips. In an ad for an automatic copying machine, a monk pretends to copy elaborate illuminated manuscripts by hand, while actually running them off on the machine. Even that symbol of evil, the devil himself, is no more than an amusing chap dressed up for a costume party in an ad for "uncandles."

Of course, not all ads are like the ones we've looked at in this chapter. Many make positive points. Certainly a great deal of public service advertising does. So do many ads for charitable organizations. The AT&T ads that urge us to telephone long distance emphasize the importance of maintaining ties among families and friends. A series of newspaper and magazine ads for Aetna Life and Casualty, an insurance company, focuses on the high cost of medical care in this country. Each ad concludes by encouraging us to take steps that may help lower costs.

Ads can perform valuable services. A few, like the Morris-the-cat ads for 9-Lives cat food, are genuinely funny.

But such ads are not common enough. Too often, advertising promotes such ideas as "Morality is silly"; or "People are constantly criticizing us"; or "Safety is going along with the crowd." It seems surprising that we accept ideas like these, and the ads that convey them, with so little question. But we do.

We are surrounded by ads, and to us, that's entirely natural. We expect that whenever a TV drama begins to get exciting, an ad will interrupt the action. We automatically assume, when the radio announcer says, "And now it's time for the weather report," that we will have to listen to two or three commercials before the report actually begins. We don't question the fact that billboards obscure once lovely views of plains and mountains.

We willingly accept the fact that some advertising affects our popular culture. For decades, children knew that Santa Claus's sleigh was drawn by eight tiny reindeer. Then a copywriter for a mail-order house invented the red-nosed Rudolph as a sales gimmick. Today, every child knows that Santa has nine reindeer. In the same way, familiar catchphrases, "Try it, you'll like it" or "They said it couldn't be done," started out as advertising slogans.

Some brand names have become part of the language too. The word yo-yo was once a brand name for a particular toy. Cornflakes, raisin bran, escalator and linoleum used to be brand names, too. *Oreo,* the trademark of a frosting-filled chocolate cookie has even taken on a slang meaning among black Americans. It refers to a black person who "sells out" to whites—someone who's black outside but white inside.

So thoroughly do we accept advertising that most of us are not particularly bothered when we spot a false or misleading ad. A 1978 public opinion poll showed that 93 percent of Americans believe that they cannot trust ads. Yet very few people in that 93 percent ever protest against advertising. Few join consumer groups or complain when they buy a product that does not live up to the claims made for it. Many of those who know that much advertising is not quite honest, but who accept it anyway, call advertis-

"But Mr. Carruthers, you said you needed forty Xeroxes."

Mr. Carruthers used our name incorrectly. That's why he got 40 Xerox copiers, when what he really wanted was 40 copies made on his Xerox copier.

He didn't know that Xerox, as a trademark of Xerox Corporation, should be followed by the descriptive word for the particular product, such as "Xerox duplicator" or "Xerox copier."

And should only be used as a noun when referring to the corporation itself.

If Mr. Carruthers had asked for 40 copies or 40 photocopies made on his Xerox copier, he would have gotten exactly what he wanted.

And if you use Xerox properly, you'll get exactly what you want, too.

P.S. You're welcome to make 40 copies or 40 photocopies of this ad. Preferably on your Xerox copier.

XEROX

Advertising can make changes in language. In this ad, the Xerox Corporation asks us *not* to change the name of a copying machine into another word for *copy*.

ing a *game*. Surely, it's a game that's sometimes played by unfair rules, they say, but that very unfairness is part of the game.

Not only do we willingly accept advertising, but many of us are eager to become part of advertising. That's reasonable, since Americans have learned that being asked to advertise for a product signifies that a person has reached the pinnacle of success. Skater Dorothy Hamill was a big winner in the 1976 Olympic Games. She immediately became a big winner on Madison Avenue, too, appearing in commercials for Short & Sassy shampoo. Other sports stars who have endorsed products include Joe Namath, Joe DiMaggio, Tom Seaver, and Billy Martin. The list is practically endless.

Success in other fields also brings requests from manufacturers for product endorsements. Actors and actresses ranging from England's Sir Laurence Olivier, to France's beautiful Catherine Deneuve, to little-known American starlets can be seen shilling products in print and on the air. Comedian Bill Cosby has advertised for Del Monte foods, White Owl cigars, Jell-O desserts, Pan Am airlines, and the Ford Motor Company. Even the respected playwright Lilllian Hellman struck an elegant pose for Blackglama mink.

Few of us will ever become famous enough to land an advertising contract. It's unlikely that a business will pay us the million dollars an insurance company paid Gregory Peck to do an ad. Still, ordinary Americans can make their way into ads.

A campaign for Ivory soap has young men and women from around the country vying for the honor of promoting Ivory on TV. Those housewives in "hidden camera" TV ads who act amazed and delighted when they discover which detergent got their clothes so white and bright are happy to be part of the School on Madison Avenue. So is the boy who brings to the beach a towel stamped with an outsize Budweiser beer can or the girl who adjusts her scarf so that the designer's name, Vera, shows clearly. Then there's the woman whose belt buckle forms the initials YSL. She's wearing an ad for the clothing and accessories of French designer Yves Saint Laurent.

A man who spends $30 to have "rally stripes" put on his car is *paying* for the privilege of advertising for an auto manufacturer. On the other hand, the 5,000 or so Volkswagen owners whose autos are covered with decals advertising everything from cereal to cigarettes to blue jeans receive $20 a month for the use of their cars. But the small payment isn't important to them. It's the fun of being a mobile ad that has caused more than 75,000 additional VW owners to apply to an ad agency to have decals put on their cars, too. "It's a great way to meet people," said one successful applicant who has learned to let Madison Avenue help him overcome his insecurities.

Advertisers know that millions of Americans want to be part of the world of advertising, and they are happy to encourage them. That's why they plan campaigns like the one using VWs or the one for Ivory soap.

Even people who don't have the luck to make it into a finished ad can become part of Madison Avenue by participating in marketing surveys. Every year, market researchers ask thousands of Americans to tell them about their likes and dislikes in consumer products. What scent do they prefer in a soap? Do they use a mouthwash? What color is it? How often do they buy a new car? What do they look for in choosing a pair of shoes? The answers to these and hundreds of other queries help ad agents decide which of a product's qualities to emphasize—and which to ignore.

Advertising people work hard to teach children to want to be part of ads as well. One summer, the Ralston Purina Company ran a series of TV ads for its Jack in the Box restaurants. The ads, which were aired in California, urged children under ten years of age to enter a "Jack in the Box sweepstakes" contest. The prize: an opportunity to appear in a Jack in the Box ad. California youngsters who took part in the sweepstakes had obviously accepted the idea

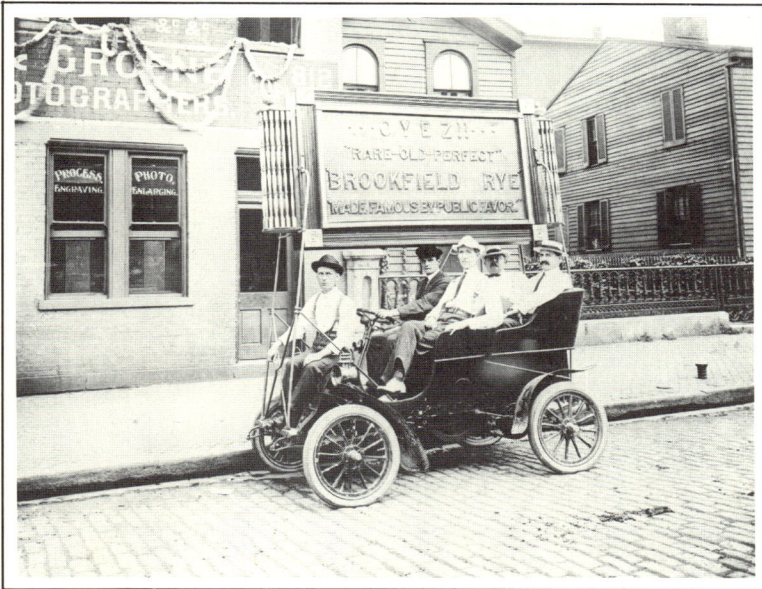

Americans have long been happy to lend themselves—and their cars—
to further the ends of the School on Madison Avenue.

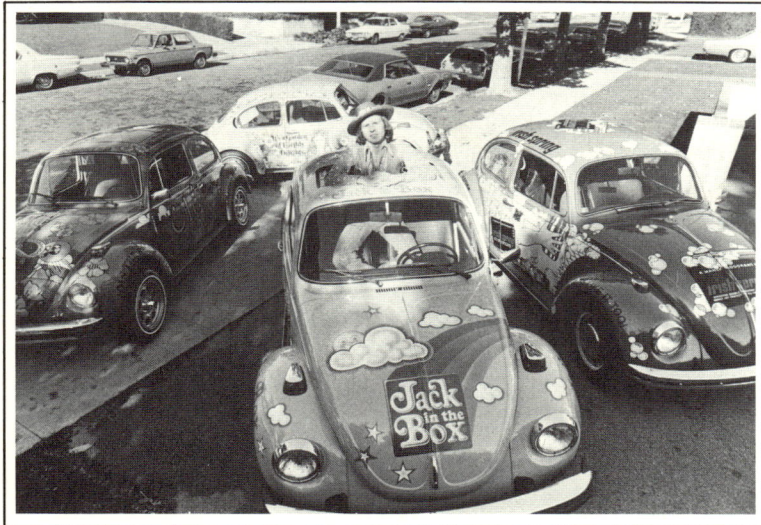

that the chance to promote a product is in itself a valuable prize.

Why does Madison Avenue bother to advertise to such young children? Surely they don't have much money of their own to spend.

That's so. But copywriters are looking to the future. They regard girls and boys as consumer trainees—people who are learning to be the buyers of tomorrow. They want to make sure that tomorrow's buyers will spend their money on the things they are advertising. "Eager minds can be molded to want your products," advised an ad aimed at getting more manufacturers to advertise to children.

The ad went on. "Sell . . . children on your brand name and they will insist that their parents buy no other."

That sentence sums up another reason why advertisers are so eager to get their messages across to children. A child is the advertiser's personal representative in the child's home. If children can be made to want certain products, advertisers believe, they will see to it that their parents buy those products.

To an advertiser, that's "kid power." To millions of Americans, it's a normal way of doing business. It's normal to entice children to watch TV reruns and then to bombard them with dozens of ads—many of which may be misleading or untruthful. It's normal to try to manipulate children, to "mold their eager minds." It's normal to teach them that happiness comes from owning material objects and that advertising can become an entire way of life.

Or if it isn't normal, we accept it as such. "In the world of commerce," says writer Joseph Seldin, "children are fair game and legitimate prey." Apparently, children are essential to the School on Madison Avenue.

Chapter 6
A Consumer Paradise?

Imagine a world in which . . .

- · people are urged to spend money they don't have
- · toys are three-dimensional ads
- · television programs are intended to be less interesting than the commercials
- · professional sports teams alter their rules to please advertisers

Sound like bits and pieces from a science-fiction writer's nightmare? They're not. All these things are happening in the United States today. They're happening as Americans learn the lessons of Madison Avenue more and more fully.

Some of us are coming to accept advertising's values and to adopt those values as our own. We are starting to put the needs of business and industry before the needs of our fellow human beings. We are changing our ideas about what we want from life and how to get it, about what our problems are and how to solve them, about our place in the world. We are beginning to change the ways we think and act as a people.

At the start of the twentieth century, for example, going into debt was considered not just unwise but disgraceful. Oh, it was all right to buy a house with a mortgage that could be paid off over ten or twenty years. And substantial, one-time purchases, such as the farmer's reaper or his wife's sewing machine, might be bought "on time." But to buy clothes, jewelry, or household goods on credit was almost universally frowned upon.

By 1920, American attitudes had reversed themselves completely. It became commonplace for families to be in debt. Automobiles, which cost far more than most people could pay in a single lump sum, played a big part in bringing about this change. So, as time went on, did electric refrigerators, washing machines, stoves, and other large appliances.

The national consumer debt grew rapidly. In 1956, it was over $28 billion. Twenty-one years later, in 1977, it had just about tripled. American families now owe billions of dollars on everything from houses and bank loans to restaurant meals and vacation trips to medicines and charitable donations.

We Americans have piled up this enormous debt because people in business and advertising have convinced us that it is better to owe money than to do without any of the shiny new products that tempt us. Having built up this debt, we cannot get rid of it. The money we are paying now for things we "bought" last year ensures that business will have enough money to produce this year's goods. And millions of us must buy on credit this year, or factories will not be able to produce goods for tomorrow.

According to Rudolph A. Peterson, former president of the Bank of America, "Debt performs a vital function in our economy and it must grow in order for the economy to prosper." Another leading banker agrees. "If everyone started spending only what he earned, it would be worse than a depression, it would be a catastrophe," he says.

Besides changing the way Americans pay for what they buy, advertising is changing Americans' ideas about what they *want* to buy. Ads try to convince us that "this year's model" is invariably better than last year's. They urge us to reach for "fast" and "easy" on the supermarket shelf without asking whether the speed and convenience of instant breakfasts and precooked dinners is worth the sacrifice of nutrition and good taste. They are training us to believe that, of fifteen nearly identical brands of mouthwash, one is best because of its particular flavor or coloring. In other words, ads are telling us to look only for surface qualities in the products we buy. They are teaching us not to examine products carefully to find out whether they are well made—or even useful.

Advertising also helps determine what products we *can* buy. Dolls are a good example of how advertising does this.

Children have always played with dolls—dolls fashioned from sticks, dolls stuffed with rags, dolls with exquisite wax or china features, dolls with soft vinyl bodies. Most dolls represented babies or very young children.

They were meant to be hugged, kissed, washed, changed, and taken for walks. They were fun to play with, and they helped teach children to become loving parents in their own turn.

Today, dolls are different. Five-year-olds play with teenaged Barbie dolls, the wardrobes of which a movie star might envy. They push a panel of Super Joe Commander's back, and Super Joe responds with a swift uppercut. They place Suntan Tuesday Taylor in bright sunshine or electric light and watch her skin darken.

Why are such dolls offered for sale? One answer, says Peggy Charren, president of a consumer group called Action for Children's Television, is that TV advertising demands them.

Ms. Charren explains. "Toys are designed to make good thirty-second messages, not to make good toys," she says. "That's why you have all these dolls that walk, talk, roll over, and so on. They can each do one thing, which looks great on TV." What about dolls' traditional role as playthings that help children learn to become loving parents? "You can't even hug the dolls because of all that machinery in their middle," complains Ms. Charren.

Other dolls are *themselves* ads. These dolls are designed and outfitted to resemble the stars of some popular TV shows. Advertisements for such dolls amount to advertising for the programs as well. For example, TV ads for a set of Charlie's Angels dolls and accessories double as ads for the program of the same name.

That's interesting, because ads for these dolls are aimed at young children. But the program upon which the dolls are based is supposed to be an adult program. It goes on the air after the evening family hour, when, in theory, youngsters are in bed.

Yet although T V executives *say* they agree that young children shouldn't see "Charlie's Angels," and although they schedule the program later in the evening, they allow it to be advertised to children through ads for the dolls. To add still more confusion, one episode of "Charlie's Angels" included a scene in which a toy maker gives each Angel a doll modelled upon herself. As the camera pans over the dolls in loving detail, the three Angels examine the toys, exclaim at how lifelike they are, and ask the toy maker where they can buy sets for young relatives. Where does the program end and the ad begin?

That's a question that could be asked about a lot of T V. Advertising is what television is all about. Unlike early newspapers and magazines, some of which banned advertising altogether, T V has always been primarily an advertising medium.

It's easy to see why. Television attracts massive audiences. When a network broadcasts the Super Bowl football game, people in about 45 percent of American homes tune in. The final episode of the blockbuster success "Roots" reached more than half of all the homes in the country. Ads aired during such programs will be seen by tens of millions of people, many times the number that would see ads for the same products in any other medium.

Of course, the costs of running ads during popular programs are enormous, too. That makes advertisers anxious for viewers to be in the right mood to pay attention to their messages and to act on their suggestions. And T V executives, aware that their profits come from the sale of advertising time, are equally eager for advertisers to be pleased with the results of their ads.

One network president put this eagerness into words: "Since we are advertiser-supported, we must take into account the general objectives and desires of advertisers as a whole. An advertiser . . . is spending a very large sum of money . . . it seems perfectly obvious that advertisers cannot and should not be forced into programs incompatible with their objectives.''

Advertisers certainly are not forced into sponsoring "incompatible" programs. Virtually everything that appears on TV is painstakingly crafted to highlight the commercials.

On television, convenient, luxurious living is the norm. Even families that are supposed to be lower-middle-class or poor are surrounded by upper-middle-class comfort. People on TV wear beautiful clothes, and they seldom appear in the same outfit twice. At the conclusion of most daytime TV shows, an announcer informs us where we can buy clothes like those the stars were wearing.

People use push-button phones. Their cars are new and rust-free, and they always start at the first try. No one ever has to hunt for a parking space. People eat and drink heartily and gain not an ounce. They hop into airplanes at a moment's notice. Their homes are spotless, although no one ever seems to dust or clean the bathtub. Teenagers have cars, motorcycles, skis, and tennis rackets. Every room has a matched set of furniture. People live gloriously on their credit cards, but we rarely see them paying bills.

The people in nearly all TV programs live in a consumer paradise. The message to viewers is clear: *Everyone* lives in a consumer paradise. Eventually, most viewers get the feeling that Americans—whether their homes are in exclusive suburbs or low-income housing projects—have sleek new cars and push-button phones and stylish clothes. By the time the ads come on, viewers are in a mood to go out and buy the same things for themselves. The ads—and

T V itself—have persuaded them that luxury is an American birthright.

Advertising determines what kind of life-style is portrayed on T V, and it determines the kinds of programs that go on the air as well. The more people who watch a particular program, the higher its "rating," and the more money network executives can charge advertisers for air time during it. So when the executives decide which programs to buy and broadcast, they select the ones they think will appeal to the greatest number of people. They choose situation comedies, or sitcoms, with story lines so simple that a four-year-old can follow them yet with enough off-color jokes to keep an adult amused. They pick police shows with the crude violence that appeals to our so-called aggressive instincts. They choose game shows that are thirty minutes of nonstop advertising.

It's simple enough for the networks to contrive to get fictional programs like sitcoms or dramas to suit the needs of advertisers, but what about programs of fact, like sports contests or news and weather programs? Are they beyond the influence of advertising?

No.

During the past few years, professional sports have bent over backwards, and bent rules, too, to please television advertisers. Pro tennis changed its scoring rules. Football teams agreed to call more time-outs to allow more time for commercials. The twenty-four teams of the North American Soccer League reorganized themselves completely so that their games could be more conveniently broadcast. League Commissioner Phil Woosnan said the reorganization would allow the teams to take greater advantage of "excellent television marketing opportunities." Major-league baseball schedules more and more night games so that sponsors can reach large nighttime audiences. One network promised viewers a quarter-million-dollar winner-take-all tennis match between Jimmy Connors and Ilie Nastase. Audiences were large, and advertisers delighted. Later, people in those audiences found out they had been tricked. Before the match began, the network had guaranteed to pay Connors $500,000 win or lose. Nastase, the loser, got $150,000.

News, too, undergoes some strange twists in the interests of its sponsors. Sometimes news stories that might offend an advertiser are played down or left out completely. More commonly, advertising influences the manner in which news is presented, especially on TV.

TV news is delivered crisply and neatly. Anchormen and -women slide easily from hard news to hard sell. On some programs, especially local news programs, reporters read ads as well as news. Often, news borders on entertainment. Stories about complex situations are dropped in favor of less important items that can be accompanied by exciting film footage. During a half-hour newscast (really a twenty-three-minute newscast, since seven minutes may be used for advertising), reporters generally include one or two light human-interest stories. The anchormen and -women may take the time to exchange a few jokes. This has been dubbed the sitcom style of news reporting, and while it may not be reporting at its best or most accurate, it does keep audiences tuned in for the next commercial.

It's said that everyone talks about the weather, but nobody does anything about it. The Albany, New York, advertising agency for a nationwide department store chain proved to be an exception. One winter, a vice-president at the agency sent a memo to radio and TV stations asking forecasters to refrain from warning people against driving during severe snowstorms. "This type of weather 'editorializing' does terrible damage to retail store sales," the vice-president wrote. "It's hard enough to create retail sales. . . . We certainly don't need air personalities discouraging them." He threatened to reduce advertising on stations that did not stop advising people of poor driving conditions.

Finally, advertising affects the overall quality of television programs. In general, they must not be too interesting, too exciting, or too funny. A vice-president at one network explains why a program must not deeply move the people watching it or ruffle their feelings in any way. "Such ruffling," he said, ". . . will interfere with their ability to receive, recall, and respond to the commercial message." In other words, the audience may spend the commercial breaks discussing the story or laughing at the jokes instead of paying attention to the ads.

The vice-president may be correct. Writer Vance Packard says that when "I Love Lucy" became TV's most popular show, its sponsor's sales dropped 17 percent. Packard and some other writers fear that when a program is so good it "overpowers" its sponsor's messages, that program has little chance of maintaining its high quality. Perhaps that's one big reason for the low overall quality of commercial television.

There's no doubt that advertising dominates TV. It probably has more effect there than on any other area of our lives. Yet its influence in other areas is growing. Advertising strongly affects the way we see ourselves as a society.

Advertising is like a distorting mirror. It shows men and children dirtying the house while women (coached by men) clean up after them. It hides nearly all the elderly but

On the set of the TV series ''The Electric Company,'' comedian Bill Cosby helps teach reading. Cosby teaches us to buy and consume, too, with ads for Jell-O and numerous other products.

a few sick or senile specimens. It also hides handicapped people, except in advertising appeals for money to combat specific illnesses. It shows us few blacks, and those it permits us to see are firmly entrenched in a white middle-class way of life. Ads show us almost no members of other minority groups, such as Spanish-Americans or American Indians.

But that's not what our society is really like! Women are just as capable as men. Children are nice people. There *are* older Americans—millions of them—and many are perfectly healthy in mind and body. Handicapped people live among us. And, as we enter the 1980s, 5 percent of the country's population is Spanish-American, and 11 percent is black.

Why does advertising ignore such facts? Because many members of racial minorities work at low-paying jobs, or can't find jobs at all, and therefore lack the buying power of middle-class whites. Because few elderly people have as much money to spend as younger ones. Because the handicapped may find it difficult to work and shop. Because many women and children are dependent on their husbands and fathers to pay their bills.

In focusing on the economic reality that the youthful, white, middle and upper-middle classes represent much of the country's consumer spending power, Madison Avenue ignores another reality: that all of us, men and women, blacks and whites, young and old, are part of the same society. What any part of our society does, wants, or feels affects the rest of us. No one group stands alone.

In advertising's distorting mirror, however, the parts of our society are isolated from one another. And advertising has a different message for each group.

To affluent whites, ads say: Enjoy yourself right now, today, immediately, by purchasing every possible kind of luxury and convenience. You're important, you must be happy and satisfied.

To blacks, ads say: A few of you will be allowed to share in the American Dream. But the rest of you—you who struggle against poverty or near poverty—will have only this tantalizing glimpse of that dream.

To the elderly, ads say: You are old and sick and forgetful. You are to be pitied or laughed at.

To the handicapped, to the minorities who are almost never seen, to the poor of all races, ads say: We're not going to bother with you.

Of course, copywriters do not deliberately put these messages into the advertising they write. But the messages *are* there because the agents must concentrate their selling efforts on the people who can and will buy—and buy. Those are the people whom copywriters must feature, and flatter, in their ads. Other people can be ignored.

But those "other people" are aware of advertising's underlying messages, too. When they pick up a newspaper or a magazine, or turn on the radio or TV, or see a billboard, or open a piece of direct mail advertising, they are reminded that millions of their fellow citizens enjoy a way of life from which they are left out. It's hardly surprising that they begin to feel resentful or that divisions between black and white, rich and poor, young and old are still so deep in the United States.

As our society creaks under the strains that advertising helps put upon it, so does our democratic political system. More and more, our political life is influenced by the techniques of Madison Avenue.

The idea of political advertising itself is nothing new. In 1838, the editor of the *Boston Daily Times* offered to sell newspaper space to any political party that wished to advertise. Readers expressed outrage at the editor's suggestion, and he countered by asking, "We advertise for individuals and associations of every kind, and why not a political party?"

Why not indeed? By the twentieth century, advertising was commonplace in election campaigns. The amount of political advertising grew as the advertising industry itself did, and by the 1950s, ads were as much a part of an election as the speeches.

Not all Americans looked upon this development with favor. In 1956, a member of the Democratic party, Adlai Stevenson, commented, "The idea that you can merchandise candidates for high office like breakfast cereal—that you can gather votes like box tops—is, I think, the ultimate indignity of the democratic process.'' Stevenson was referring to the ''merchandising'' of the Republican party's candidate for president, Dwight Eisenhower. It's true that the Republicans did a lot of political advertising in the 1956 campaign, which Eisenhower eventually won. But so did the Democrats, on behalf of their losing candidate—Adlai Stevenson.

If Stevenson disapproved of political advertising in 1956, he would have been appalled by it now. Today's candidates carry on media blitzes that become more intense with every election. As soon as a man or woman decides to run for office, he or she almost automatically hires an ad agency to prepare commercials. The commercials can be expensive. In a presidential election, a candidate's advertising costs may be as high as $10 million.

Politicians and the people who work on their campaigns are quick to defend the use of so much political advertising. They point out that the country is too large to permit a candidate to visit every city and state in person. Only through advertising can candidates make themselves and their views known to voters. Ads give every citizen the opportunity to see the opposing candidates, to listen to what each has to say, and to make a choice.

But others ask whether watching a thirty- or sixty-second TV ad allows people to tell what candidates are really like or to make an informed judgment about their views. Ads for political candidates—like ads for other products—rely on snappy slogans, tricky camera angles, music, and wit to get their messages across. A well-done ad can make a weak candidate look as good as, or better than, a strong one. It can make a crooked politician look honest or a foolish one seem wise.

Many people suggest that all spot advertising really does is impress the candidate's name on people's minds. The more times a candidate's ad is repeated, the more likely voters are to remember the name—and to vote accordingly. This means that in order to win, all candidates would have to do would be to buy more advertising time and space than their opponents.

Certainly, many people in advertising see our election process in this light. Says adman Rosser Reeves, "I think of a man in a voting booth who hesitates between two levers as if he were pausing between competing brands of toothpaste in a drugstore. The brand that has made the highest penetration on his brain"—that is, the candidate whose ads he remembers best—"will win his choice."

If Reeves's picture of the average voter is accurate, our democracy may be headed for trouble. It's one thing for a person to buy Crest instead of Gleem because she's seen more Crest ads, but it's quite another for her to vote for a president or a senator or a mayor simply on the basis of the number of ads she's seen.

It would be serious enough if Madison Avenue's influence on politics stopped with the preparation of slick ads and TV spots. But it doesn't. It's becoming more common for an advertising agency to plan a candidate's entire political campaign—starting with telling him what to tell the voters he believes in.

The first step is research. Just as researchers question consumers to learn their preferences in soaps and cars, so they question voters to find out what they want in a candidate. In 1975, after Jimmy Carter decided to run for president, he commissioned research to learn what kind of person Americans wanted in the White House. The answer, researchers found, was "a man we can trust."

Researchers told Jimmy Carter that voters wanted trustworthiness in 1976. Admen fashioned a massive campaign around that theme, and Carter won the election.

At once, "trust" became Carter's campaign theme, and for months he hammered home the idea that he was a person the country could depend upon. Voters bought the idea and elected Carter. But were they getting a trustworthy president? Or were they getting one whose researchers had hit upon something Americans wanted and whose admen had concocted an effective campaign?

Is it enough, in a democracy, to vote for a label or a theme? Is it enough to make a choice among candidates who may not know what they stand for until researchers tell them? Is it safe to allow Madison Avenue to play so great a role in the country's political affairs?

We could ask similar questions about advertising's influence on other aspects of our public lives. In the 1980s, the country is going to face serious problems. The time is coming when Americans will have to make some difficult decisions—decisions about how to deal with our growing energy needs, what to do to protect the environment, whether to keep unsafe products off the market, and so on.

But will we?

There is, for example, the question of a possible energy shortage. Will the United States one day run out of the oil, coal, and gas it needs to heat its homes and schools, to fuel its cars and planes, to run its factories, and to supply its electricity? The weight of evidence indicates that the answer is yes.

By the late 1970s, this country was importing 15 million barrels of oil *every day*. (A barrel holds 42 gallons of oil.) Yet even that was not enough. The country was also bringing in oil by pipeline from Alaska. Coal and natural gas were needed to meet our energy demands as well. World energy supplies won't last forever if they are used at such a rate. During the last century, we have consumed resources that nature took millions of years to build up. Estimates say that if the United States had to stop importing oil from other countries, we would exhaust our Alaska reserves in just two years.

One day, all our current oil resources will be used up. No one is sure when that day will be. Some predict it will be soon—within ten or twenty years. Others say it may not happen until the year 2050 or 2100.

Then there are those who say it probably won't happen at all. They include some of the people who run the country's huge oil and gas corporations as well as some auto manufacturers, and leaders of other American industry. They assure us that talk of an energy crisis is nonsense. Americans will always have all the energy they want.

Advertising for this point of view is increasing. The Mobil Corporation spends $21 million annually on an advertising and public relations program designed to convince us that we don't have to sacrifice in order to save energy. Queries the headline in one Mobil ad, "Should U.S. energy policy make me feel guilty about my lifestyle?"

Mobil's response is a resounding no. The ad suggests reasons people may have for preferring to drive large cars or station wagons. It points out the difficulties in planning for public transportation in rural areas. It urges everyone to take that dreamed-of-vacation trip. Finally, it raises the specter of what might happen if people make the mistake of anticipating an energy crunch. The government may force people to give up their private homes to live in energy-saving apartments, cautions the ad. "Or how about two families to an apartment?"

This is just one of many ads with a similar theme. The ads seem to be having their desired effect. Public opinion polls show that most Americans think an energy shortage is highly unlikely. So we go on, burning more energy every year, and hastening the time when we must face the energy problem head on.

For that time will come. Whether it comes in ten years or fifty years is not the point. Someday, we will run out of the energy resources we have learned to rely upon. When that day arrives, our lives will change drastically. If we get to work now and start to plan for those changes, they will be easier for everyone. But if we don't take the energy problem seriously until the last drop of oil has been squeezed from the world's last oil well, the results will be devastating. That is just the most obvious danger of allowing ourselves to be persuaded by this kind of advertising.

A more subtle danger is that such advertising tells us it's all right to put off facing difficult situations. It encourages us to avoid looking squarely at our problems and making the tough decisions that must be made. Before long, we may forget that real problems call for real solutions. We may believe that a sincere-sounding ad is in itself a solution.

Corporation executives and their ad agencies already seem to believe that. They know that many Americans are worried about pollution and other environmental problems, and they want to convince us that they are equally concerned. So they run ads stressing that concern.

However, such ads nearly always conclude that, deep as the industry's concern is, environmental problems are much more involved and complicated than we ever imagined. In fact, the problems are so complex that we must put in a good deal more time and thought before taking any action—or requiring industry to spend a sizable share of its profits on working out solutions.

This attitude is what Senator Henry Jackson of Washington has called the public relations response to problems. In the early 1970s, Jackson estimated that it would cost industry $8 billion a year for five years to clean up its pollution. At the time, industry was spending only a fifth of that amount. That leaves a $32 billion gap between PR image and reality.

The gap between image and reality exists in our everyday lives, too. In our heart of hearts, for example, we know that cigarette smoking is bad for us. We're aware of the American Cancer Society statistics: Smoking is the direct cause of 80,000 American deaths from lung cancer each year; it is the direct cause of 15,000 yearly emphysema deaths; it helps bring about an unknown number of deaths from heart attacks and other illnesses. Overall, says the National Cancer Institute, smoking contributes to about 325,000 deaths in the United States every year—three smoking-related deaths every five minutes.

That's the reality. The image is different. Cigarettes don't mean suffering and death, but glamour and maturity. Smoke Marlboro, and know the healthy outdoor life of the western range. The Silva Thins smoker is a trim and elegant woman. The handsome, tanned blue-eyed Salem smoker doesn't let *anything* get in the way of his pleasure. That's the image, and the tobacco industry spends nearly half a billion dollars a year to promote it. The money is well spent. Fifty-three million Americans smoke, and the number of teenaged smokers—who can be counted upon to buy cigarettes for the next forty or fifty years—is growing.

Image triumphs over reality in the matter of alcoholic beverages, too. We are aware that alcohol is an addictive drug. We know that at least 6.5 million Americans are alcoholics and that 8,000 American teenagers die in drunk-driving accidents each year. Yet most of us cling to the Madison Avenue image of drinking as glamorous, sophisticated—and harmless.

We ignore other realities of liquor advertising. Some ads urge us, not just to drink, but to drink *more*. One beer is "the beer to have, when you're having more than one." "Glass after glass" is the way to enjoy alcohol. Perhaps the ultimate beer drinkers are those who prefer Schlitz. They're happy to give up the tools of their trades, their tal-

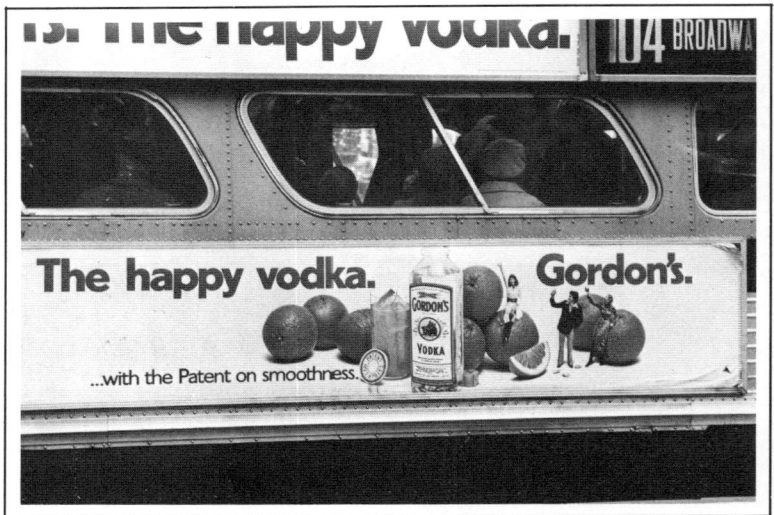

On Madison Avenue, alcohol doesn't make you sleepy, drunk, or hung-over. It doesn't affect your driving. It has nothing to do with alcoholism or other diseases. It's "happy."

ents, their professional skills—*anything*—as long as they can keep their "gusto," their Schlitz.

We ignore the way the liquor industry tries to tap new markets. Because research shows the heaviest users of hard liquor are white, adult males, one company is trying to entice nondrinkers, especially blacks, young people and women, with "Hereford's Cows." These are sweet beverages that taste like soda pop, but which contain 15 percent alcohol. Ads for another company push a line of wine-based cocktails: "It's more fun than the Pepsi challenge." Unlike hard liquor, wine-based drinks may be advertised on TV and, in many parts of the country, sold in supermarkets.

Advertising for these drinks is aimed at eighteen- to thirty-four-year-olds. In many states, it's not legal for anyone under the age of twenty or twenty-one to drink. That doesn't stop distillers and agents from urging teenagers to experiment with alcohol.

We allow a number of dangerous products to be advertised and sold. The low-calorie sugar substitute saccharin may cause cancer, but it's still on supermarket shelves. Hair dyes are available, although they, too, have been linked to cancer. Highly sugared foods that may lead to tooth decay and weight problems are urged upon people of all ages, particularly upon children.

Many of the machines we buy and use are unsafe. Power lawn mowers kill and maim many users every year. But, notes a government report, the cost of adding safety features to the mowers isn't worth it. Scientists have known since the very early 1970s that aerosol spray devices contain an ingredient that destroys the atmosphere's ozone layer and allows harmful rays from the sun to pass through. Yet the federal government waited until April 1979 to place a ban on aerosols.

The needs of business come first. And their primary need, in the opinion of businesses and advertising people, is unceasing growth. Unceasing growth means making more money year after year after year. And that is possible only if people buy more goods every year.

That's why advertising is vital to American business. In order for business to grow, Madison Avenue must convince us that we want more and more luxuries, that we long for things we've only just heard of, and that we should spend our money before we earn it. Madison Avenue has succeeded at its job. Most of us accommodate ourselves willingly to business's needs.

Where will it end? A science-fiction theme suggests one answer. The pressure to buy and use up consumer goods becomes so great that it is made the burden of the poor.

The poor are forced to work day and night to wear out clothes and toys, to use up what they bought today so they can buy more tomorrow. That keeps factories humming, and the economy booming. In this vision of the future, only the privileged rich are entitled to purchase and consume no more than they really need. Only the rich may lead simple lives with time to visit friends, read books, plant a garden, or listen to music.

This vision isn't likely to come to pass. A more probable scenario is that the world will run out of natural resources and that we will have to abandon our mad drive to produce and consume. Or that people in the poorer nations of Asia, Africa, and South America will one day tire of watching us use up more than our share of the world's riches and rise against us to take some for themselves.

It's always possible, as well, that we will step back and take a look at ourselves and the way we live. We may see what we are like and what we are becoming.

And we may decide to do something about it.

Chapter 7
Truth
in Advertising

Doing something about advertising means trying to keep advertising fair, honest, and moral. It means regulating advertising.

Few would dispute the idea that advertising needs regulation. But people do argue over who should do the job. Many Americans think it should be up to state and federal governments. The men and women who work on Madison Avenue disagree. They say that advertising is perfectly capable of regulating itself.

As evidence, people in advertising point to the industry's seventy-five-year history of self-regulation. In 1903,

John Adams Thayer became the first adman to speak out strongly against fraudulent advertising. Two years later, a group of advertising executives formed the Associated Advertising Clubs of America, afterward known as the Advertising Federation of America, and launched a movement for honest advertising.

By 1911, the movement was going strong. The federation adopted the slogan "Truth in Advertising" and formed "vigilance committees" to monitor advertising in various parts of the country. Through the pages of *Printers' Ink,* the trade paper of the advertising world, the federation campaigned for state laws making it a crime to advertise untruthfully. Federation members even wrote a model law to help state governments draw up their own statutes. Under this law, a "person, firm, corporation, or association" whose advertising contained "any assertion, representation or statement of fact which is untrue, deceptive, or misleading" would be guilty of a misdemeanor. A misdemeanor is punishable by a fine or by up to twelve months in jail.

The federation's push for truth in advertising met with fair success. Within a few years, thirty-eight states had passed *"Printers' Ink* laws." The vigilance committees had reorganized themselves into the Better Business Bureau, the aim of which was to see that businesses lived up to their advertising claims.

Today, the Better Business Bureau has offices in many cities. Often these offices are combined with a city's Chamber of Commerce. They are places where consumers can go to complain when they think they've been misled by false advertising or been tricked into buying poor-quality goods. The Better Business Bureau investigates a complaint, and if it seems valid, bureau members try to get the consumer's money back.

Until the 1900s, there was little regulation of advertising. Advertisers could make wild claims—and they didn't have to back those claims up as they must today.

However, the bureau has no legal power to force an advertiser to make good on false claims or to replace inferior merchandise. All it can do is try to convince the advertiser that, in the long run, dishonest business practices only hurt the business community. Many businesses, though by no means all of them, accept this reasoning and make amends to cheated consumers.

The Better Business Bureau has another self-regulatory tool. This is its National Advertising Division.

The NAD listens to complaints, not about individual businesses in separate cities, but about national advertising aimed at millions of people. Like the local Better Business Bureaus, the NAD checks out the complaints it hears, and when an advertiser cannot back up a claim, the NAD asks for a change in the advertising or for an end to it altogether. Like the Better Business Bureau, the NAD lacks legal authority.

One complaint that came to the NAD concerned ads for Gillette's Good News twin-blade disposable razor. According to Gillette, "You don't have to worry about nicks and cuts" with this razor. The NAD thought that statement might give shavers "a false sense of security," and Gillette agreed to reduce its claim. Another complaint had to do with Mobil 1 synthetic motor oil. Ads for the oil said it could clean better than detergents in other motor oils. The NAD asked Mobil for proof of the oil's cleansing ability and, when Mobil was unable to provide it, asked the company to drop the ad. Mobil agreed.

Still another recent case dealt with a Planters peanut butter ad that claimed, "Now Planters peanut butter is better . . . better than the leading peanut butter." Asked by the NAD for proof, Planters cited a test in which a majority of consumers praised Planters' taste and "spreadability." Not proof enough, ruled the NAD, that Planters was superior to all other brands in virtually every way. Planters changed its advertising.

Advertising media are also involved in advertising self-regulation. It's network officials themselves who decide how much air time to sell to advertisers. Early in 1978, executives at the country's three major commercial TV networks decided to increase the number of ads their networks carried. The executives met no opposition from the FCC because there are *no* legal limits on the amount of advertising time a station or network can sell. However, the executives did run into opposition from the president of the Westinghouse Broadcasting System, which owns stations affiliated with (that carry the programs of) each of the three networks.

Westinghouse president Donald H. McGannon criticized the networks for steadily increasing the amount of time sold to advertisers. He let it be known that his stations would not make any additional time available for commercials. Instead, McGannon said, Westinghouse would donate more free time for public service announcements. Newspapers, too, have put some limits on advertising. Two papers, the *Los Angeles Times* and the *New York Times,* stopped accepting ads for hard-core pornographic movies. Cigarette advertising does not appear in the *Christian Science Monitor,* the *New Yorker, Scientific American,* or the *Reader's Digest.*

Does self-regulation work? Certainly, cutting down on amounts of advertising and keeping tabs on exaggerated claims are a good idea. Yet getting rid of ads for some X-rated movies in a couple of newspapers or forcing a merchant to return $5 or $10 to a customer who's been cheated doesn't make much of a dent in the real problems with advertising.

Self-regulation has done little to keep advertisers from lying, directly or indirectly, about their products. That's because the NAD deals with false advertising on a case-by-case basis. It has no authority to tell advertisers once and for all that they *must* stick to the truth.

Self-regulation has not succeeded in getting advertisers

to place the good of society ahead of their own profits either. It has never tackled the problem of whether or not cereal makers should be allowed to tell three-year-olds that a breakfast food consisting of nearly 50 percent refined sugar is good for them. It has not addressed the question of whether TV program quality should be lowered so the sponsors' ads will look better. It has not asked whether teenagers should be tempted by drinks that taste like soft drinks but that contain two-and-a-half to five times as much alcohol per ounce as beer. It has not pondered the morality of turning children into mini-salespeople in their own homes. It does nothing to try to stop advertising from becoming an even greater part of our lives—taking more time from TV programs, slipping into movie theaters, or intruding into our homes by means of an increasing number of "junk phone calls," telephone advertising messages.

What it boils down to, many people say, is that trying to cure the ills of advertising through self-regulation is like trying to cure a broken leg by sticking a bandage on it. Self-regulation just isn't enough. It should be up to the government to do the job.

Over the years, the government has taken some actions to regulate advertising. In 1906, Congress passed the Pure Food and Drug Act. That law made it a crime to sell unsafe foods or medicines. Since it was a federal law, however, the Pure Food Act applied only to products that were transported across state lines.

Actually, the law didn't even succeed in stopping the interstate trade in dangerous products. During the 1930s, several people wrote books exposing the fact that dangerous products were still being advertised and sold. One of the best-known books was *100,000,000 Guinea Pigs,* by

Arthur Kallet and F. J. Schlink. Kallet and Schlink charged that "A hundred million Americans act as unwitting test animals in a gigantic experiment with poisons, conducted by the food, drug and cosmetic manufacturers." Advertising, the authors went on, was guilty of promoting the manufacturers' deadly products. Advertisers disputed Kallet and Schlink's claims, but in 1938 the book helped prod Congress into passing a new law to limit the further use of dangerous substances in products advertised to the American public.

Since 1938, Congress has passed other consumer protection laws. In 1965, it voted to require cigarette manufacturers to put a health hazard warning on all cigarette packages. Later, Congress banned cigarette advertising on radio and TV. Other federal laws passed since the mid-1960s seek to protect Americans from unsafe cars, impure meats and poultry, dangerous radiation, and so on.

Some state governments have moved on behalf of consumers and against some advertising practices. Oregon and California outlawed aerosol sprays long before the federal government did. California lawmakers decided that autos sold in their state would have to be less polluting, even if it meant that California drivers would not get as many miles to the gallon of gas as before. A Maine law seeks to eliminate billboard advertising except on stores.

It's no coincidence that a number of state and federal consumer protection laws have been passed during the last fifteen years. The laws were written as a result of pressure from consumer advocates—men and women who speak out on consumer issues.

One familiar consumer advocate is Ralph Nader. In 1965, Nader published *Unsafe at Any Speed,* a book that accused American automakers of knowingly designing, manufacturing, advertising, and selling cars that were not safe to drive. It was unsafe cars, Nader said, not bad drivers, that were causing many of the nation's auto accidents.

At first, people paid little attention to *Unsafe at Any Speed*. No one wanted to hear that those lovely, luxurious cars streaming out of Detroit were highway menaces. Even most book reviewers refused to write about the book in newspapers and magazines. "I wouldn't touch this book with a ten-foot pole," one magazine reviewer told Nader's publisher. Why not? A newspaperman from Texas supplied the answer: "With all our automobile advertising? You must be crazy."

As it turned out, it wasn't the publisher who was crazy. In January 1966, the country's leading auto manufacturer, General Motors, hired a private detective to investigate Nader. The detective's assignment: look into Nader's private life—his politics, health, drinking habits, friends— and find some damaging facts to use as a weapon to silence his criticism.

GM's blackmail plan backfired. The news media learned of it and broke the story. The United States Senate ordered the president of GM to come to Washington, D.C., to explain the auto company's action. The publicity shocked Americans into taking Nader's charges seriously—and into demanding that the government do something to protect them from unsafe autos.

The GM uproar eventually died down, and Nader went on to become one of the country's most successful consumer advocates. In 1968, he organized a corps of students to come to Washington and help him investigate various consumer problems. The students, promptly nicknamed Nader's Raiders, change from summer to summer. But

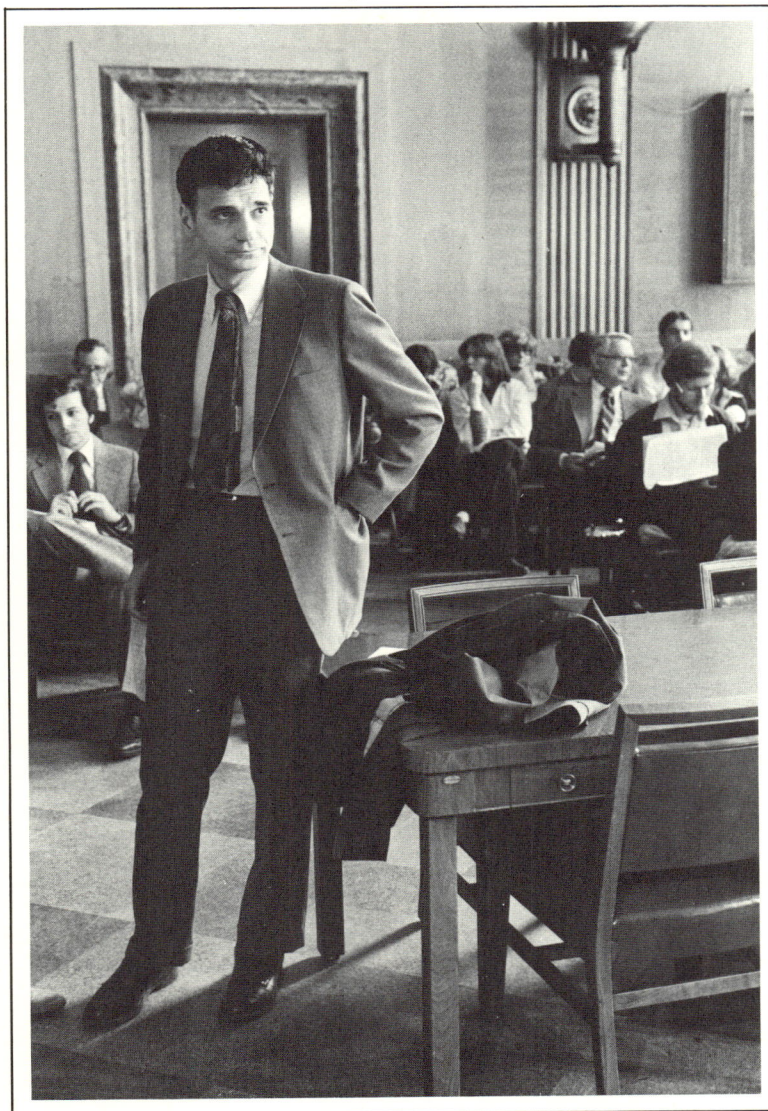

Ralph Nader's *Unsafe at Any Speed* led first to some dirty doings by General Motors executives. Later, it gave impetus to the consumer protection movement.

their mission, to uncover areas in which new consumer protection laws are needed, remains constant.

Nader and his Raiders are not the nation's only consumer advocates. The government employs hundreds of men and women whose job it is to protect American consumers.

Some of them work for the United States Postal Service. Postal inspectors in each state act on complaints from people who feel they have been duped by mail-order advertising. The inspectors examine complaints, and if they can gather enough evidence against the advertisers, they take action. That action may consist of getting a court to order an advertiser to stop making a particular claim. Or it may mean having the post office refuse to deliver any more mail to the advertiser's business address—something that seems certain to put an end to that money-making scheme.

The Federal Communications Commission is another federal agency charged with the regulation of advertising. For example, the FCC has suggested an advertising "fairness doctrine." Under it, radio and TV stations must offer free time for messages that counter certain kinds of advertising. Before Congress ended TV cigarette advertising, for instance, the FCC required stations to broadcast public service ads that warned of the dangers of smoking. More recently, the FCC ordered a Washington, D.C., station to carry ads paid for by a consumer organization called Energy Action. Energy Action ads disputed oil company claims that the companies always place the public welfare before their own financial interests.

Consumers can also appeal to the Federal Trade Commission when they discover what they believe to be unfair advertising. The FTC was set up by Congress more than sixty years ago to protect Americans from deceptive business practices and untruthful advertising.

One consumer group that has repeatedly lodged complaints with the FTC is Action for Children's Television—ACT for short. Based in Massachusetts, ACT was formed in 1968 by several mothers who were worried about the way that television and its advertising were affecting their children.

Since 1968, ACT has petitioned the FTC to forbid manufacturers to advertise to children for toys, vitamin pills, cereals, candy, and firecrackers. Advertising such products to children is unfair, ACT claims, because children are not old and wise enough to watch the ads critically. They do not understand that many products—like sugary foods—are not good for them and that others—like firecrackers and some toys—might cause serious injury.

For years, ACT petitioned the FTC in vain. Over and over, the commission refused to issue stricter rules about advertising to children. However, ACT did convince the manufacturers of some products, including firecrackers and vitamins, to withdraw their ads.

By 1977, there were signs that the FTC might be about to take a stronger stand. The new FTC chairman, Michael Pertschuk, spoke favorably of ACT's work. He promised that the commission would soon issue a report on the group's latest petition, which called anew for an end to the advertising of candy and heavily sugared cereals for children.

Chairman Pertschuk kept his promise. The FTC made its report public in February 1978. The 340-page report recommended eliminating all advertising aimed at children under eight years of age. It suggested banning ads for the most heavily sugared foods to children age twelve and under. It advised requiring advertisers to counter their own commercials with ads that promote health and good nutrition. Finally, the report concluded that the FTC should go

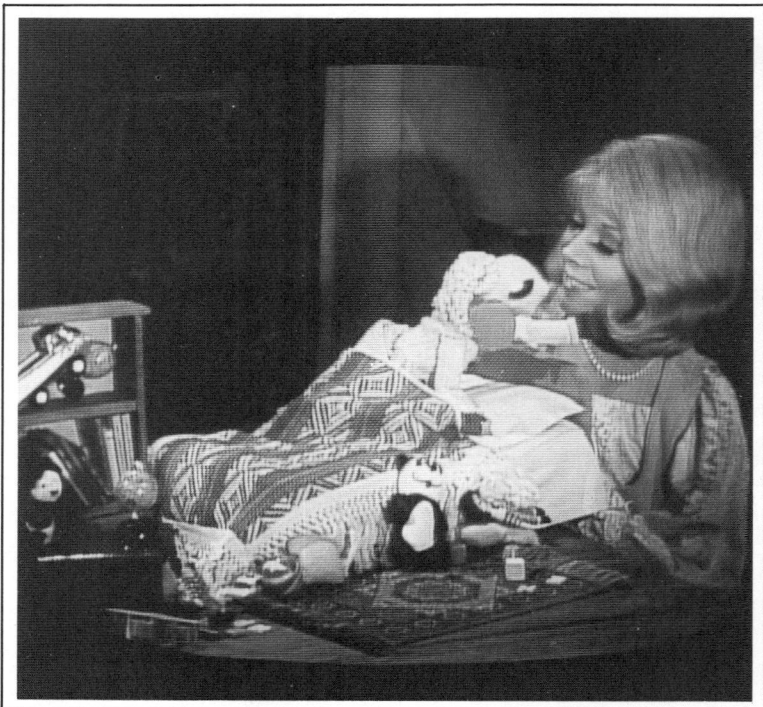

THE NATIONAL BROADCASTING
COMPANY, INC.

Lots of sweet snacks mean poor nutrition. That's Lambchop's message to young TV viewers. This series of public service ads, also featuring puppeteer Shari Lewis, comes from NBC-TV.

ahead with a fifteen-month series of hearings on the effects of TV advertising to children. Doctors and other experts would be asked to testify at those hearings.

The people who manufacture toys, candy, and cereals, and those who advertise them, reacted furiously to the FTC report. Even before it was officially released, the Kellogg cereal company bought two full pages in the *New York Times* to defend its cereals as "worthwhile" and "nutritious." The ad backed up Kellogg's claim by quoting studies—some of which were made by Kellogg's itself—showing that children could indeed benefit from eating its products.

Claiming that sugary cereals are nutritious was only part of Kellogg's two-pronged attack on the FTC and the consumer movement. The other part centered on Madison Avenue's often-stated conviction that any criticism of advertising is a threat to democracy and the American way of life. As a member of the agency that prepares Kellogg advertising put it, "Even if . . . a child perceives children in television advertising as friends, and not as actors selling them something, what's the harm? All a parent has to say is, 'Shut up or I'll belt you!' "

Of course, most people in advertising and business do not share this man's child rearing philosophy. But most are convinced that government must not be permitted to regulate advertising. As we saw earlier, many business leaders and advertisers see their work as democracy in action. According to them, government regulation will one day strangle free enterprise—the "democracy of the marketplace."

How? A government ruling that a particular product is dangerous and must be taken off the market limits people's right to choose the things they want to buy. Laws that forbid certain kinds of advertising to children would deprive advertisers of their freedom of speech, advertisers say.

This point of view was reflected by Kellogg president William E. LaMothe in a speech to the Association of National Advertisers. LaMothe told association members, ". . . We must shout in defense of our right to communicate with our audience, be they children, the elderly, minorities, disadvantaged, rich, poor, black or white." LaMothe's listeners agreed that advertising was facing a battle for its rights.

Critics of advertising deny that an attack on false or misleading advertising, or on advertising that is unfair to its audience, is an attack on the entire advertising industry. They dismiss the notion that criticism of advertising is an attack on business itself or on democracy. Instead, they say, their criticism is a natural response to past and present advertising abuses, abuses that even some people in the advertising industry admit exist. It is part of an effort to see that the public benefits from honest and useful advertising—and is protected from ads that are neither.

Chapter 8

A Last Lesson

One lesson remains for students at the School on Madison Avenue. That lesson is summed up in the warning sounded by the people of ancient Rome: *caveat emptor*. In Latin, the language of Rome, *caveat emptor* means "Let the buyer beware."

Let the buyer beware . . . let the buyer be aware . . . that a little of the advertising we see and hear is dishonest and an outright fraud. Some of it is stupid or vulgar. Much of it is garish, noisy, intrusive, repetitious, and ugly. Nearly all of it encourages the overconsumption of natural resources and ignores the environmental damage that often goes along with overconsumption.

However, the buyer should also be aware of advertising's pluses. Advertising can tell us about a new book that may inspire and uplift us. It can let us know about a terrific sale. It can offer us a chance to save money on cents-off coupons. It can inform us about genuinely useful new products.

Advertising does help keep our economy going. It helps create jobs. It can allow manufacturers to charge lower prices for mass-produced goods (although the costs of advertising and packaging tend to raise prices). Advertising for charities, educational institutions, medical foundations, and similar groups encourages people to contribute millions of dollars a year to worthwhile causes.

Furthermore, advertising is branching out in new ways that should eventually benefit all Americans. In June 1977, the Supreme Court, the nation's highest court of law, ruled that lawyers must be permitted to advertise their services. Before that, state laws had kept lawyers and other professional men and women from telling the public about their qualifications or their fees.

Following the Supreme Court ruling, lawyers in one state after another began advertising, especially in newspapers and on TV. Most are delighted with the result—more business. Many consumers are delighted, too. Seeing and hearing the ads give people an opportunity to pick and choose lawyers. The ads also let them know ahead of time how much their lawyers are going to charge.

As soon as lawyers' ads began appearing, so did ads for other professionals. Dentists tell prospective patients what they charge for a set of false teeth. Doctors post their charges. Drugstores put up price lists so customers can comparison shop—and perhaps save money on expensive medicines.

American Tourister

"Dear American Tourister: You're great on unscheduled flights." Janet Clay, Bernville, Pa.

DOYLE DANE BERNBACH
FOR AMERICAN TOURISTER

Ads can be stylish and witty. This one earned an award for the agency of Doyle Dane Bernbach.

Such advertising can mean lower prices. One study showed that the cost of eyeglasses dropped by about one-fourth in states that began allowing opticians to advertise their services.

But let the buyer always be aware of the other side of the advertising coin. Every ad—whether it's for a lawyer or a light bulb, a dentist or a deodorant, a charity or a chili sauce—has one aim: to persuade us to do something. Most often, that "something" involves spending money.

Before we do spend, we should think clearly about what it says.

What this commercial is trying to sell you won't make your breath any sweeter, your clothes any whiter or your acid indigestion any better. It'll just make you more human.

1. (Music under)

2. Announcer's voice: if you take away . . .

3. . . . man's novels . . .

4. . . . his poems . . .

5. . . . if you take away . . .

6. . . . his drawing and painting . . .

7. . . . if you forget about his theatre and movies . . .

8. . . . if you take away man's music . . . (sfx out) . . .

9. . . . if you take away his crafts . . .

10. . . . if you take away all his arts . . .

11. . . . you just might find man up a tree. Take the time to stop, look and listen.

12. Art is for man's sake.

BUSINESS COMMITTEE FOR THE ARTS, INC.
1270 Avenue of the Americas, New York, N.Y. 10020

BUSINESS COMMITTEE
FOR THE ARTS, INC.

Not all advertising focuses on people's problems, shortcomings, or insecurities. Some recognizes that there's more to life than bad breath and tension headaches.

Does the ad for this detergent contain the careful wording of a permissible lie? If so, the detergent probably is no better than many similar brands. It may be more expensive, though.

Does an ad for a body builder or a bust developer sound too good to be true? Then it almost certainly is. Read the fine print. That "simple exercise" will doubtless be included in any book on physical fitness. And the wonderful cream or miracle protein may be right on your supermarket shelf—at a lower price.

Does a mail-order ad instruct you to call a toll-free number to place your order? That can be a clue that post office inspectors have found that the advertising is a fraud and have advised cutting off mail delivery to the advertiser's address.

Does a hidden camera interview convince you that Mrs. Average Housewife believes this cake mix and no other will make her husband happy? Think again. It's a good bet that the only people from whom the camera is really hidden are in the viewing audience.

Does the ad for a stereo tape deck make the product sound good—but leave you feeling not quite sure that it is? Then check it out with reports from Consumers' Union or Consumers' Research, Inc. These groups, which are supported entirely by consumers, thoroughly test a wide variety of products and publish the results. You can find their publications in the library.

No matter how aware we buyers are, though, all of us will be taken in by misleading ad claims at some time. What then?

The first step for any consumer who feels cheated is to complain directly to the advertiser. Often, this brings quick results. The problem may turn out to have been due

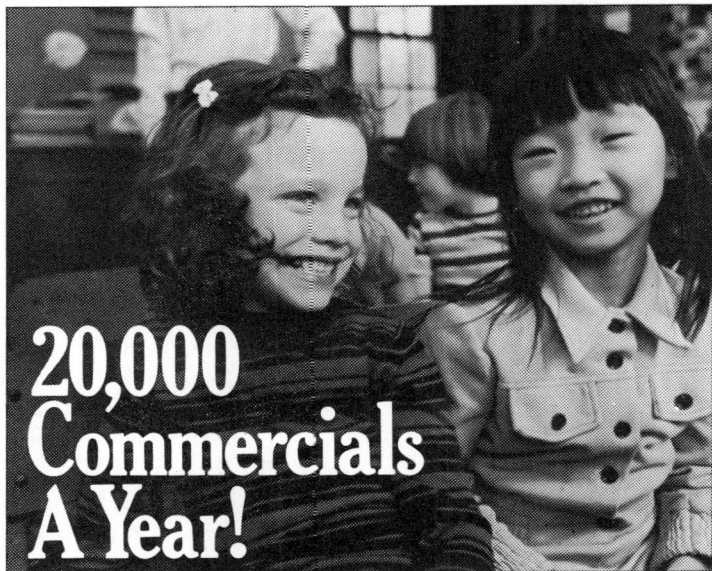

Ads can warn against ads. TV journalist Bill Moyers examines children's advertising and the FTC hearings—and a newspaper ad tells people when and where to watch.

to a misunderstanding. In other cases, when advertisers really have been dishonest, a firm stand may convince them that making restitution—giving back the consumers' money—is better than facing possible legal action.

What if the advertiser just ignores a complaint? Get in touch with the nearest Better Business Bureau or Chamber of Commerce. You will be asked to complete a form outlining your side of the story. If your complaint seems to be justified, someone at the bureau will act on it. But don't forget that the Better Business Bureau has no legal standing.

A state consumer agency, however, does have that standing. Most states have consumer agencies. If your state is one of them, you'll find the agency listed under the state's name in the telephone book for the state capital. Or you can get the number through information. Don't expect a state consumer agency to rush right out and prosecute a dishonest advertiser, though. The agency's first step will be to try to persuade the advertiser to make restitution. Only if all efforts at mediation fail will the case be turned over to an attorney for court action.

Going to court is a last resort, and there's a reason for that. It's expensive. It takes a lot of time. Even lodging a complaint through a business association like the Better Business Bureau takes time and effort.

Perhaps the best way to guard ourselves against deceptive advertising and dishonest business practices would be to establish a national consumer protection agency. Such an agency could see that rules for business and advertising are the same in every part of the country. It would have the legal power that self-regulatory groups lack. It would not have to deal with business problems on a case-by-case basis.

A national consumer protection agency seemed close to becoming a reality early in 1978. Congress was considering a bill that would have created an agency. But last-minute pressure from business and industry convinced a majority of congressmen and -women to vote against the bill.

So our best protection is still—ourselves. It's up to us to examine the advertising we see and hear and to judge for ourselves how deserving it is of our attention. It's up to us to be aware, to beware.

Caveat emptor. It's the final, and most important, lesson at the School on Madison Avenue.

Bibliography

Baker, Samm Sinclair. *The Permissible Lie*. Cleveland, Oh.,
    and New York: The World Publishing Company, 1968.
Barnouw, Erik. *The Sponsor*. New York: Oxford University
    Press, 1978.
Eisenberger, Kenneth. *The Expert Consumer*. Englewood
    Cliffs, N.J.: Prentice-Hall, Inc., 1977.
Glatzer, Robert. *The New Advertising*. New York: The Citadel
    Press, Inc., 1970.
Packard, Vance. *The Hidden Persuaders*. New York: David
    McKay Company, Inc., 1957.
Rowsome, Frank, Jr. *They Laughed When I Sat Down*. New
    York: Bonanza Books, 1959.
Seldin, Joseph, J. *The Golden Fleece*. New York: The Macmil-
    lan Company, 1963.
Wood, James Playsted. *The Story of Advertising*. New York:
    The Ronald Press Company, 1958.

Index

Italic page numbers refer to captions.

126